羽 化
Eclosion

比提雅 著
By Bithiah

旧事已过，都变成新的了

The old has passed away
Behold，the new has come

加拿大国际出版社
Canada International Press

羽化

书名：羽化
作者：比提雅
出版：加拿大国际出版社
印刷版 ISBN: 978-1-998479-64-1
电子版 ISBN: 978-1-998479-65-8
2025 年 12 月 加拿大第一版
2025 年 12 月 第一次印刷
© 2025 版权所有，翻印必究

Book Title: Eclosion
Written By: Bithiah
Published by: Canada International Press
Print version ISBN: 978-1-998479-64-1
EBook version ISBN: 978-1-998479-65-8
First Edition in Canada: Dec. 2025
First Printing: Dec. 2025

谨将本书献给你

I dedicate this book to you

一路走来，如果你经历在黑暗中的挣扎，要向上举目，因造你的神眷顾你，祂把你的眼泪装在祂的皮袋里，保护你的性命，搭救你的脱离恶人的手，救赎你脱离罪的辖制，救护你的脚不跌倒、使你在生命光中行在祂面前。

Along the way, if you have experienced struggles in the darkness, lift up your eyes, for the God who created you cares for you. He has put your tears into His bottle. He preserves your life, delivers you from the hand of the wicked, redeems you from the bondage of sin, and keeps your feet from falling, that you may walk before God in the light of life.

"我也为此劳苦，照着祂在我里面运用的大能尽心竭力"

(歌罗西书 1:29)

"For this I toil, struggling with his energy that he powerfully works within me"

(Colossians 1:29)

羽化

前 言

　　"神造万物，各按其时成为美好，又将永生安置在世人心里。然而神从始至终的作为，人不能参透。我知道世人，莫强如终身喜乐行善；并且人人吃喝，在他一切劳碌中享福，这也是神的恩赐。我知道神一切所做的都必永存；无所增添，无所减少。神这样行，是要人在祂面前存敬畏的心。现今的事早先就有了，将来的事早已也有了，并且神使已过的事重新再来"

（传道书 3:11-15）

　　"耶稣又对门徒说：'所以我告诉你们，不要为生命忧虑吃什么，为身体忧虑穿什么；因为生命胜于饮食，身体胜于衣裳。你想乌鸦，也不种也不收，又没有仓又没有库，神尚且养活它。你们比飞鸟是何等地宝贵呢！你们哪一个能用思虑使寿数多加一刻呢？这最小的事，你们尚且不能做，为什么还忧虑其余的事呢？你想百合花怎么长起来；它也不劳苦，也不纺线。然而我告诉你们，就是所罗门极荣华的时候，他所穿戴的，还不如这花一朵呢！你们这小信的人哪，野地里的草今天还在，明天就丢在炉里，神还给它这样的妆饰，何况你们呢！你们不要求吃什么，喝什么，也不要挂心；这都是外邦人所求的。你们必须用这些东西，你们的父是知道的。你们只要求祂的国，这些东西就必加给你们了。你们这小群，不要惧怕，因为你们的父乐意把国赐给你们。你们要变卖所有的周济人，为自己预备永不坏的钱囊，用不尽的财宝在天上，就是贼不能近、虫不能蛀的地方。因为，你们的财宝在哪里，你们的心也在那里″

（路加福音 12：22-34）

　　小孩子通常不需要为每天的生活担忧，他们知道有父母会为他们预备一切；但他们出于本能会想独占自己所爱的东西，不愿意与他人分享。因为我们是″在罪孽里生的，在我母亲怀胎的时候就有了罪″，所以我们从出生就懂得自私自利，自欺欺人，自以为义，厌恶被批评，更不要说承认自己有罪。″光来到世间，世人因自己的行为是恶的，不爱光，倒爱黑暗，定他们的罪就是在此″（约翰福音 3：19）。感谢神在基督耶稣里饶恕了我们，″如今，那些在基督耶稣里的就不定罪了。因为赐生命圣灵的律，在基督耶稣里释放了我，使我脱离罪和死的律了。律法既因肉体软弱，有所不能行的，神就差遣自己的儿子，成为罪身形状，作了赎罪祭，在肉体中定了罪案，使律法的义成就在我们这不随从肉体、只随从圣灵的人身上。因为，随从肉体的人体贴肉体的事；随从圣灵的人体贴圣灵的事。体贴肉体的，就是死〞（罗马书 8:1-6a）。〞你们死在过犯罪恶之中，祂叫你们活过来。那时，你们在其中行事为人，随从今世的风俗，顺服空中掌权者的首领，就是现今在悖逆之子心中运行的邪灵。我们从前也都在他们中间，放纵肉体的私欲，随着肉体和心中所喜好的去行，本为可怒之子，和别人一样。然而，神既有丰富的怜悯，因祂爱我们的大爱，当我们死在过犯中的时候，便叫我们与基督一同活过来〞

（以弗所书 2:1-5a）

改革开放后，越来越多中国人移居国外，对于第一代移民，在语言的挑战和文化的冲击下，大部分人过得都满了艰辛，虽然中国人在外国都是公认的勤劳守法，但因为太过于专注在自己的家庭和财富上，所以很少有精力投入在所住国家的政治生活中，因为没有习惯参与选举，也就意味着成了当地政府不重视人群，很多移民抱怨权益得不到维护，但如果不能成为政府的选票来源，任何族类都会是同样的遭遇，即便能带来社会价值，在国外也无法和选票相提并论。一部分人会在被边缘化的现实中愤世嫉俗，报复社会，亦或自我毁灭；另一部分人不以为然，满足于自己的社交圈子，两耳不闻窗外事，一心只在己事中；还有一部分人幡然悔悟，融入本地的生活，追求信仰，回报社会，寻求参政，利己利民。

有着三千年深厚文化的中国，也是饱经沧桑的中国，在儒家、道统和皇权、政统中养成含蓄内敛和谨小慎微的中国人尽管走出了国门，但心还守着某些固有的东西。老一辈人因为资源匮乏而养成的节俭带到了国外，有时候会引发媒体爆料，比如中国人疯抢免费食品或者赠品而彼此大打出手，比如中国人开着名车去救济场合领取自己并不真需要的东西，并在经过挑选后，将部分丢进垃圾桶……等等引发社会的不满和鄙夷。新一代人在老一辈人的环境中耳濡目染，以及本地教育和文化体系的洗礼，双重夹击中多多少少会有些无所适从的无力感和自卑感。在国外的中国人面临的境地和中国当下的处境是相同的问题---没有信仰作为坚实基础，中华民族很难彻底摆脱外患内忧。经济实力只能提供给人满足外面的虚荣，内里的平安喜乐惟独来自鉴察人心的神。"既是这样，还有什么说的呢？神若帮助我们，谁能敌挡我们呢？"

(罗马书 8:31)

羽化

Foreword

"He has made everything beautiful in its time. Also, he has put eternity into man's heart, yet so that he cannot find out what God has done from the beginning to the end. I perceived that there is nothing better for them than to be joyful and to do good as long as they live; also that everyone should eat and drink and take pleasure in all his toil-this is God's gift to man. I perceived that whatever God does endures forever; nothing can be added to it, nor anything taken from it. God has done it, so that people fear before him. That which is, already has been; that which is to be, already has been; and God seeks what has been driven away" (Ecclesiastes 3:11-15)

"And he said to his disciples, 'Therefore I tell you, do not be anxious about your life, what you will eat, nor about your body, what you will put on. For life is more than food, and the body more than clothing. Consider the ravens: they neither sow nor reap, they have neither storehouse nor barn, and yet God feeds them. Of how much more value are you than the birds! And which of you by being anxious can add a single hour to his span of life? If then you are not able to do as small a thing as that, why are you anxious about the rest? Consider the lilies, how they grow: they neither toil nor spin, yet I tell you, even Solomon in all his glory was not arrayed like one of these. But if God so clothes the grass, which is alive in the field today, and tomorrow is thrown into the oven, how much more will he clothe you, O you of little faith! And do not seek what you are to eat and what you are to drink, nor be worried. For all the nations of the world seek after these things, and your Father knows that you need them. Instead, seek his kingdom, and these things will be added to you. Fear not, little flock, for it is your Father's good pleasure to give you the kingdom. Sell your possessions, and give to the needy. Provide yourselves with moneybags that do not grow old, with a treasure in the heavens that does not fail, where no thief approaches and no moth destroys. For where your treasure is, there will your heart be also'" (Luke 12:22-34)

Children usually don't need to worry about their daily needs, because they know their parents will provide everything for them. However, they instinctively want to possess what they love and are unwilling to share with others. This is because we are "brought forth in iniquity, and in sin did my mother conceive me." So, from birth, we are self-centered, self-deceiving, self-righteous, averse to criticism, and much less likely to admit we are sinful. "And this is the judgment: the light has come into the world, and people loved the darkness rather than the light because their works were evil" (John 3:19). Thanks be to God in Jesus Christ forgave us, "There is therefore now no condemnation for those who are in Christ Jesus. For the law of the Spirit if life has set you free in Christ Jesus from the law of sin and death. For God has done what the law, weakened by the flesh, could not do. By sending his own

Son in the likeness of sinful flesh and for sin, he condemned sin in the flesh, in order that the righteous requirement of the law might be fulfilled in us, who walk not according to the flesh but according to the Spirit. For those who live according to the flesh set their minds on the things of the flesh, but those who live according to the things of the Spirit. For to set the mind on the flesh is death"(Romans 8:1–6a). "And you were dead in the trespasses and sins in which you once walked, following the course of this world, following the prince of the power of the air, the spirit that is now at work in the sons of disobedience-among whom we all once lived in the passions of our flesh, carrying out the desires of the body and the mind, and were by nature children of wrath, like the rest of mankind. But God, being rich in mercy, because of the great love with which he loved us, even when we were dead in our trespasses, made us alive together with Christ"(Ephesians 2:1–5a).

After China's Reform and Opening-up, more and more Chinese people moved abroad. For the first generation of immigrants, life was often full of hardship due to language challenges and cultural shock. While Chinese people are widely recognized as hardworking and law-abiding overseas, they are often so focused on their families and wealth that they have, they have little energy to get involved in the political life of their host countries. Because they are not accustomed to participating in elections, they become a demographic that local governments do not prioritize. Many immigrants complain that their rights are not protected, but if they cannot become a source of votes for the government, any ethnic group would face the same situation. Even if they contribute to society, their social value can't compare to the power of votes abroad. A portion of people who feeling marginalized, become cynical and vengeful towards society, or self-destructive; another group remains indifferent, content with their own social circles, uninterested in what happens outside their personal lives; there are still some who awaken, choose to integrate into the local community, seeking faith, giving back to society, and pursuing political participation for their own benefit and the benefit of others.

China, with its profound three-thousand-year cultural, is also a country that has been through many hardships. Shaped by Confucianism, Taoist traditions, imperial authority, and political systems, Chinese people have developed a reserved, cautious, and restrained character, even after moving abroad, their hearts often holds on to certain ingrained behaviors. The frugality developed by the older generation due to a lack of resources is often brought overseas, which sometimes leads to negative media reports, for example, Chinese people fighting over free food or promotional items, or driving luxury cars to food banks to pick up things they don't truly need, only to discard parts of them in trash after picking and choosing… These behaviors often spark social dissatisfaction and contempt. The new generation, influenced both by their elders' environment as well as the local education and cultural systems, finds themselves caught in a double bind, often feeling a sense of helplessness and inferiority. The predicament Chinese people face abroad is the same issue China currently faces: without a solid foundation of faith, the Chinese nation will finds it difficult to completely escape both internal and external troubles. Economic strength can only provide external vanity; inner peace and joy cam only come from God who examines the human heart. "What then shall we say to those things? If God is for us, who can be against us? " *(Romans 8:31)*

羽化

目录

第一章 幼虫

"曾有死亡的绳索缠绕我，匪类的急流使我惊惧，阴间的绳索缠绕我，死亡的网罗临到我"

（诗篇 18:4-5）

　　冉竹被姐姐的惊呼声惊醒，之后院子里繁杂的脚步声掺杂着哭泣声，让冉竹那颗小小的心脏快要跳了出来，穿上衣裤和鞋子跑出房门看见大人们都已经进到姥姥的房间了。"姥姥……"冉竹不知所措地看着躺在床上一动不动的姥姥，喉咙里胡乱地发出声响。大人们不许冉竹贴近姥姥的尸体，可她真的想还和往常一样依偎着姥姥，听姥姥讲那些过去的事情，累了就用小脸蹭蹭姥姥的脸，姥姥就会紧紧抱住她，用鼻尖贴着她的小鼻尖说："我的小猪猪（猪猪和竹竹发音相同）要睡觉觉啦。"冉竹最爱的就是用小脸贴着姥姥的脸，在姥姥呼吸之间的温暖气息里睡去。冉竹记得有一次和姥姥躺在院子里枣树荫下的躺椅上，有排成整齐 V 字形的大雁队伍经过。冉竹问姥姥为什么大雁要离开，姥姥说他们去找他们的姥姥呀，冉竹抱紧姥姥说："您可不要学大雁的姥姥丢下大雁们飞走，我不知道要去哪里找到您。"姥姥说："有一天我也必须得飞走，我的小猪猪要乖，要做勇敢的小朋友"。冉竹的小脸贴着姥姥的脸，四行泪滑落。

　　冉竹的出生是一个意外。冉景明和杜若因为已经有了四个子女，加上工作繁忙，复杂的社会关系也让他们心烦意乱，尤其是杜若。冉竹的姥爷是个生意人，姥爷姥姥曾经有过六个子女，最年长的女儿杜至，杜若是最年幼的，他们两姐妹之间本来有四个弟兄，因为出天花都夭折了，所以杜至需要招赘。杜至年长杜若 21 岁，杜至的大女儿出生的时候正好杜若出生，杜家那年特别热闹。杜若生得美貌俊秀，杜家夫妇自从四个儿子不在了，这才得了安慰，父母的宠溺里渐渐长大的杜若越发俊美，伴随着一起长大的还有骄傲自负。因为姐姐杜至生了五个女儿，没有生儿子，所以杜若也需要招赘。冉竹的爸爸冉景明，趁着年轻，孤身一人来到杜家居住的城市闯荡，在冉竹姥爷的商行谋了份差事。冉景明温和儒雅俊美，人也聪明，所以常被邀请到杜家做客，每次冉景明都不想离开杜家，因为他对杜若十分着迷，冉景明入赘杜家顺理成章。婚后的杜若在冉景明的宠爱里渐渐将骄傲自负发挥到了极致。每天目睹着被杜若折磨到快奔溃的冉景明，他岳父给了冉景明一幅字："有无相生，难易相成，长短相形，高下相盈，音声相和，前后相随，恒也"。 冉景明一生都宠爱着骄横跋扈的杜若，足以证明那幅字是入了他的心，并且有了功效。那幅字在后来的兵荒马乱里不知去向，不知去向的还有很多金元宝和其他值钱的物件，杜家就这样渐渐衰落了。很多年以后，从新西兰回国探亲的冉竹和爸妈也早已和解，甚至他们还会一起聊很多。有一次冉竹说起到她正在读的圣经里的几个章节，特别是谈到哥林多前书 13 章时，冉景明突然恍然大悟似的说："过去你姥爷给过我一幅字，仔细琢磨起来人类是有共通的智慧的，神从一本造出万族的人，住在全地上，这话是真的。"

说回冉竹的出生是一个意外这件事，冉景明和杜若因为已经有了四个子女，加上工作繁忙，复杂的社会关系也让他们心烦意乱，尤其是杜若。她已经不能承受再多一个孩子的麻烦，所以冉景明想再要个孩子的时候，杜若拒绝得很彻底。然而天意非人意能摆布，杜若怀上了第五个孩子，这对于在家里很少不能遂愿的杜若来说是难以接受的，她把心里的愤怒、怨恨、不满……所有消极情绪都发泄给那个无辜的胎儿，杜若的心里最希望这个孩子是不到期而落的胎，归于无有。在这样残酷的环境中孕育的冉竹异常叛逆，就连出生的时候也是先把一条腿伸了出来，好不容易把腿推进去，推拿到头朝下，结果出来的是一个半透明紫色的东西，吓坏了在场的人。如果不是冉竹的大表姐在她出生的时候已经是经验丰富的妇产科主任亲自接生，冉竹应该会被当成怪物立刻被消灭掉。大表姐经常告诉冉竹她出生的时候不守规矩倒行逆施，好不容易推拿到头朝下，却因为旋转过程中造成脐带缠绕住了脖子，加上羊膜囊没有破裂，任何一种都能导致胎儿窒息，如果不是她接生，凭着经验立刻剪断脐带，剪开羊膜囊，倒提着冉竹拍打她直到听见哭声，冉竹应该不会活着，对此冉竹心里是没有感激的，因为她厌恶生出来。冉竹相信她妈妈也不会感谢这个和自己同龄的外甥女救活了冉竹，因为她厌恶怀上她。杜若不喜欢冉竹，除了当初是不自愿怀上的，还有就是出生的时候让她经历了从未有的苦楚，但杜若也是忐忑的，因为相信她怀孕时满口是咒骂苦毒，所以冉竹必定是来报仇的。冉竹是怨恨杜若的，这或许是从胎儿时的经历，但她是不可能知道胎儿时自己的经历，这种怨恨在一次冉景明和杜若吵架时，冉景明列举杜若多宗罪时提到其中一件事后到达了顶峰。冉景明指责杜若经常出差不顾家，在冉竹还很小的时候连续出差好些天，冉竹每天抱着妈妈常在家里穿得一件夹袄站在大门口不吃不喝也不肯进屋，冉景明对这个倔强得像一头小驴的女儿无计可施，每次都要等冉竹困得睡倒在地上，冉景明才能把她抱回到屋里。" 杜若听了这件事后倒是对冉竹开始友好起来，后来在冉竹远走他乡的时候还特意把那件夹衣送给冉竹做个念想。冉竹绝对不相信这件事，这是对坚强的她的一种羞辱，冉竹坚决认为是爸爸编造的，冉竹根本不需要妈妈，正如她相信妈妈同样也不需要冉竹一样。这也是为什么从懂事起，冉竹就特别黏着姥姥的原因，当然冉竹是真心爱姥姥的，因为在她小小的世界里只有姥姥是那个"不稀罕其他东西，只稀罕她的小猪猪"的人。尽管冉竹的二哥和小哥每次出去玩都会带上她，那个时代里男孩子们的战争游戏充满了残酷，他们三人经常伤痕累累，脏兮兮地回到家，本以为家是可以避风的港湾，但每次等待他们的都是更猛烈的暴风骤雨。所以当初冉竹并不觉得两个哥哥是真的喜欢她，而是认为他们只不过为多一个垫背的，当然心里的芥蒂在成长的过程中如同身体的伤疤一样，尽都脱落了。

冉竹想念姥姥。大雁飞过的时候，冉竹都会仰着脸在心里默默请求大雁能带上自己，因为只有它们才会每年都不忘记去找它们的姥姥，它们飞得那么高，一定能看见姥姥在的另一个更美好的地方。院子里那棵枣树的树荫下的躺椅上经常是五表姐大刺刺地躺着，时不时盯着冉竹露出鬼魅的笑容。大姨和姨父去世的时候其他四个表姐都已经结婚搬出去住了，只有五表姐虽然到了适婚年龄还未遇到适合的人，所以仍然住在同一个院子里。五表姐能歌善舞，不喜欢正经工作，只爱到处找些表演的活动，找不到节目的时候就待在家里看些闲书，其中不乏好些男欢女爱的内容。有一年暑假的一天午后，大人照常去上班，孩子们也去学校，冉竹因为感冒发烧只好待在家里，五表姐看书看得起兴，无处释放，就跑到病恹恹躺着的冉竹身边一脸邪淫地说："你想不想知道你爸妈干了些什么生出你来的吗？"冉竹很厌恶地回答说根本不想被生出来。突然她的嘴被五表姐的嘴堵住了，同时五表姐的手伸进了冉竹的内裤，惊惧迅速爬满了冉竹的全身，在那个炎热的盛夏午后，冉竹却冷得浑身发抖，这下可挑起了五表姐的强烈欲望，发疯得压在冉竹的身上扭动，一边说着："看把你兴奋得都发抖了，你一定很喜欢这样吧。"病痛加上惊惧让冉竹昏了过去，醒来的时候眼前白晃晃刺得冉竹用手盖在眼皮上，那一瞬间，冉竹突然很开心，她以为自己是死了，去到了天堂，到了那个圣洁光明的地方。"哎呀，你可终于醒来啦！"五表姐那熟悉的声音把冉竹拉回了地狱。冉竹挣扎着要起来逃跑，被赶来的护士和不知从哪里冒出来的爸妈摁在床上，冉竹惊恐地不能言语，不知道从哪里爆发出来的力量，冉竹的尖叫声波强烈到可以撕开世界的画皮。依照五表姐给医生和冉竹的爸妈所表述的情况---冉竹发高烧昏迷开始说胡话，幸亏五表姐当时在家，在脑子就烧坏之前赶紧送冉竹去了医院。医生建议冉竹的父母，最好让冉竹休学一段时间。小哥看着在家蔫蔫的冉竹心里不好受，正好他同学家的猫生了一窝小猫，所以要了一只带回家，冉竹抱着这一团毛茸茸，哭得泣不成声。

　　毛球是冉竹小猫的名字，休学期间毛球给冉竹的生活增添了一抹暖光。回到学校的冉竹很沉默，她不再和同学们一起玩耍，也没有再参与两个哥哥和男孩子们的战争游戏。冉竹希望能用把自己孤立起来去对抗恶意。课下的冉竹在操场上一圈一圈的绕行，好几次被足球或者其他什么莫名飞行物砸到，她也不停下来，有一次飞来的足球狠狠地砸在她脸上，冲击力把她抛在了地上，她躺在那里看见很多脚向她奔来，人声嘈杂，尘土飞扬。冉竹被送去医院，脸被砸歪了，好在颧骨没有骨折，不过医生发现冉竹的面部骨骼发育不完全，甚至下颌角几乎没有成型。冉竹再次休学，每天去医院做面部电针灸半小时，护士扎好针并且通上电流后告诉冉竹，最佳促进面部肌肉活动的电针灸时间是半小时，所以冉竹需要在接近时间呼叫护士来停机。病房里只有设备的声音，护士你不呼叫就不会出现，安静得让冉竹想永远待在这里。电流嗡嗡的声音里冉竹沉睡，一个多小时后醒来感觉面部麻木。第一天冉竹惊慌失措的呼叫护士，担心会不会留下后遗症，护士坚定地回答不会，这让冉竹每天带着电流能睡得安心，这成了后来冉竹失眠的第一个原因。深夜时的冉竹睡得越来越少，醒着的时候冉竹开始写自己也不懂的诗，小哥非常欣赏，要拿去帮她投稿，冉竹拒绝了，这世界和其上的都和她不再有关联，冉竹的世界在那个盛夏的午后碎了一地。直到冉竹到了新西兰，在一个金秋明媚的周天午后，她坐在户外褪了色的木椅上读圣经，她读的是诗篇 18 篇，当读到 16 节："祂从高天伸手抓住我，把我从大水中拉上来"。继续到 19 节："祂又领我到宽阔之处；祂救拔我，因祂喜悦我。" 阳光细细碎碎透过树叶在她脸上蹦蹦跳跳，曾经的过往一幕幕浮现，她惊喜地发现心里没有了抗拒、怨恨、苦毒……甚至她心里满有喜乐，冉竹全身心感谢神，欢欣充满了她，冉竹知道的世界被重新建立了。

第二章 化蛹

"有一个少年人，名叫犹推古，坐在窗台上，困倦沉睡。保罗讲了多时，少年人睡熟了，就从三层楼上掉下去；扶起他来，已经死了"

（使徒行传 20:9）

　　毛球死了，尸体被人用重物砸过，冉竹盼望毛球没有任何的骨折，她希望毛球在另一个更美好的地方，骨骼完全，精力充沛，欢然奔跑。冉竹安静地埋了毛球，没有一滴眼泪。五表姐终于出嫁了，冉竹安静地参加了婚礼，没有一丝情绪。冉竹终于不怕一早自己出去跑步了。天蒙蒙亮，有些凉，路上的人很少。冉竹跑到一个拐角处看见了路边放着一个纸盒子好像在动，冉竹凑近看见有个白色的好像微型猪的小东西在里面，冉竹四下里想找个人问问，赶巧有个跑步的大爷经过，冉竹赶紧追上去请大爷帮忙看看，大爷是个热心肠，跟着冉竹来到纸盒边，冉竹问大爷这是小猪还是小狗，因为长得像猪，自己可不想养猪。大爷笑得眼泪都掉出来了，回答说哪会有这么小的猪，当然是狗啦，应该是刚出生，眼睛还没睁开呢，这么小，又冷又饿应该活不下去的。冉竹听得心都抽紧了，抱起纸盒说一定会活下来的，一定会。冉竹跑回家，二哥那时候刚大学毕业在家准备着开始新工作，冉竹着急要准备去学校，只能叫醒二哥，简单讲了遇见小狗的过程，现在重要的是怎么让小狗活下来。二哥毕竟年长而且读了更多的书，所以很快去找到了外甥女留在家里的奶瓶，然后冲了奶粉，并且很专业地滴在手背上测试了温度，当奶瓶凑到小狗的面前时，或许闻到了奶香，小狗跌跌撞撞地扑向奶瓶，二哥帮小狗含到了奶嘴，还没等冉竹和二哥压抑住心里的欢喜，小狗就被呛得咳嗽起来，小小的身体不停地发抖，冉竹突然就奔溃了，拿起书包发了疯得冲出家门。放学后回到家的冉竹看见二哥正在和桌子上走得东倒西歪的小狗玩耍，二哥告诉冉竹他在大表姐以前住的房间里找到了个针管，简单消了毒就用来往小狗嘴里注射奶，二哥还说小家伙不停地吃，他一停下来小家伙就用小鼻子拱他，难怪当初冉竹认为是猪呢，事实证明真的和猪没什么两样。久违的笑意终于重新出现在冉竹的嘴角。冉竹也很感激二哥再没提起那天清晨她发了疯一样夺门而出的事，其实她很想告诉二哥曾经发生的惊惧事件，但她没有说。真相必须要成为秘密，一旦说出来，可能会被取消正常生活的权力，甚至会被关进精神病院。

笑傲是冉竹小狗的名字，笑傲给冉竹的生活带来了很多的欢乐。每天放学回家，笑傲都会冲上来抱住冉竹不放开，最初笑傲只能抱住冉竹的小腿，后来笑傲慢慢长高，冉竹慢慢停止长高，就成为了拥抱。长大的笑傲比冉竹重，所以每次笑傲冲上来之前，冉竹都要扎好马步以防摔个仰八叉。场景经常是冉竹还没到院门口就听见笑傲奔跑过来的风声，推开院门前冉竹先扎好马步，门开的瞬间，笑傲已经张开双脚扑过来给冉竹一个大大的拥抱。下雨天让冉竹多了烦恼，因为等待她的是笑傲热情的带着雨后湿泥的双脚，为了不破坏他们见面的仪式感，冉竹把雨伞换成了雨衣。笑傲死后，雨天冉竹再没有打过伞也不穿雨衣，算是一种记念笑傲的仪式吧。

冉景明和杜若不喜欢之前的毛球，也不喜欢后来的笑傲，他们严格要求冉竹，要等到全家结束用餐后，剩下的食物才可以拿去喂养她的猫猫狗狗。以前冉竹经常会在周末去菜市场，问卖鱼的商贩要些卖不掉的很小的鱼给毛球改善伙食，冉竹心里觉得很对不起那些没机会长大的小鱼。后来的笑傲因为刚生下冉竹捡回来的，眼睛还没有睁开，所以每天放学回家，冉竹都会把笑傲拿到书桌上一边写作业，一边和笑傲玩。按理说看不见应该会很谨慎，可是笑傲不会按理出牌，七扭八歪，东倒西歪，跌跌撞撞，冒冒失失，好多次径直冲向桌边，虽然冉竹的及时阻止得以悬崖勒狗，但总是惊得冉竹一身冷汗，所以冉竹索性连吃饭也转移到了书桌上，为此冉景明和杜若对笑傲的不喜欢升级成了讨厌。他们经常会正吃着饭的时候突然发作，尤其是杜若，她会叫喊着冉竹："快回到饭桌上来！"这种时候冉竹会迅速吃完饭，拿着空碗往厨房走去，经过饭桌的时候有四道冷冷的目光让冉竹脊背发凉。冉竹吃饭很快得益于杜若总是纠正冉竹拿筷子的方式，以至于冉竹坚决只用汤勺吃饭后，才停止了这场没有硝烟的战争。

笑傲十多天大的时候，有次吃饭的时候杜若再度发作叫喊冉竹，冉竹迅速吃完饭拿着空碗去厨房，等她回到房间的时候，笑傲已经从书桌摔到了地上，平日的冉竹离开书桌前都会把笑傲放回窝里。冉竹惊慌失措的呼叫二哥，担心会不会留下后遗症，二哥坚定地回答不会。这并没有让冉竹每天带着内疚能睡得安心，这成了后来冉竹失眠的第二个原因。冉竹睡得越来越不踏实，总是不停爬起来检查笑傲还有没有在呼吸。好在笑傲没有意外，不过冉竹发现笑傲越来越呆头呆脑，甚至半个多月过去了眼睛还没睁开。二哥安慰说没事的，笑傲本来就呆头呆脑只会吃，而且才半个多月，或许满月了才睁眼呢。这事以后，总是担心笑傲会遇到什么不测，放学后的冉竹一路奔跑到家。体育老师看见奔跑中的冉竹，第二天找到她的班主任希望冉竹能参加学校体育队，冉竹拒绝了，不过班主任倒是每次学校运动会都在没有征求冉竹同意的情况下给她报了名。冉竹知道自己没有能力与班主任对抗，所以每次都会参赛。除了校体队的，没有其他人是冉竹的对手，班主任因为奖牌的缘故，对冉竹很满意。有一天奔跑回家的冉竹发现笑傲和平时不一样，但有什么不一样冉竹也搞不清楚。冉竹叫了二哥来，二哥开心地说，笑傲睁开眼睛啦。冉竹这才回过神来，笑傲一直用两颗又黑又亮圆圆的眼睛盯着她看，冉竹喜极而泣。得见光的笑傲让冉竹不用再每天奔跑回家，能看见的笑傲密切关注冉竹的一切活动，在家里寸步不离冉竹，为此冉景明和杜若对笑傲的讨厌升级成了憎恨。为避免冲突，冉竹几乎只待在自己房间。有天冉竹吃饭的时候发现笑傲盯着碗流口水，冉竹突然领悟笑傲应该可以吃固体食物了，于是开启了冉竹一勺，笑傲一勺的用餐模式。每天舀起的还有冉竹曾经碎了一地的世界。

　　笑傲长得很快，冉竹停止成长，而且日渐消瘦，这倒成了冉竹的最佳借口脱离班主任强加给她的校运会，所以她告诉冉景明和杜若自己需要更多专注学业，没有多余的气力为校运会准备，看着日渐瘦弱的冉竹，冉景明告诉冉竹的班主任以后不许冉竹参加校运会。之前校运会拿到奖牌冉竹没有过得胜的感觉，这次体会到了。那个年代高三不学新的知识，主要是复习准备高考，所以可以不用每天去学校，这样一来，冉竹和笑傲在一起玩得时间多了。冉景明不止一次警告冉竹要抓紧备考，不要玩物丧志。冉竹每次都坚定地回答到："请不要把笑傲物化！"这让冉景明忍无可忍。有一天学校模拟考试结束回家的冉竹到院门口了也没有听到笑傲奔跑过来的风声，推开门没有张开的双脚，没有大大的拥抱。院子里很安静，没有一丝声响，冉竹的脑袋开始嗡嗡作响，继而轰鸣到震耳欲聋。二哥在他们那里的一所高校任职，校址离家远，所以搬去校职工宿舍楼住了。冉竹用尽全力控制住手指不要抖得太厉害，才能准备放到电话盘正确号码上，终于拨完了二哥学校的电话号码，电话那头传来嗡嗡的回铃音，冉竹的心快提到嗓子眼了。接通的电话那头背景里很吵，冉竹声音发抖地念着二哥的名字，或许冉竹的声音太小，或者电话那头太吵，接线员好像听不清楚冉竹的声音，所以很大声地问你找谁？冉竹的脑袋又开始嗡嗡作响，继而轰鸣到震耳欲聋。对方挂断了电话，冉竹仍然死死握着听筒不放，直到听筒里发出刺耳的长鸣声。冉竹没有去过二哥的住处，一是校职工宿舍楼不允许会大声叫嚷的物种进入，比如鸡鸭鹅狗。不过学校里的双职工，会获准在职工宿舍附近的空地上盖窝棚养他们大嗓门的鸡鸭鹅狗，当然养蔬菜瓜果、花花草草这样安静的物种也可以。二是二哥每个周末都会回家来看望爸妈，陪冉竹笑傲一起玩。笑傲消失后的周末二哥没有回来，冉竹再次拨打二哥学校的电话，没有人接听，冉竹想起来周末学校是放假的。两周后的周末二哥回来见到冉竹就哭了，告诉冉竹三周前周末回家的时候，爸爸要他把笑傲送出去，送得越远越好。二哥学校有几家双职工同事在自家地里盖了房子养狗，所以他想不如就带笑傲回去学校，一是考虑不是送别人，等冉竹高考结束就可以再送回家；二是想着毕竟自己在学校每天都可以看见笑傲，周末回家可以告诉冉竹笑傲的日常。笑傲在二哥同事家里不吃不喝，同事也没有特别留意笑傲，只是喂自家狗的时候多添些食物而已，直到有一天同事发现躺在地上的笑傲没了气息，才惊慌失措地拉了二哥去。二哥告诉冉竹他每天去看笑傲，笑傲都会伤心得像个丢了心爱玩具的孩子一样看着他眼泪汪汪，二哥说他每天都很煎熬。冉竹僵直得站着一动不动，冉竹恨平时一勺一勺喂笑傲，造成笑傲除了这种方式就不吃东西的后果。冉竹记起笑傲到家第一天，二哥说它和猪一样能吃，冉竹希望笑傲在另一个更美好的地方能和猪一样，多多地吃。冉竹不知道自己是怎么拿着汤勺在院子里不停地砸着，落日的余晖洒在她脸上，冉竹哭得撕心裂肺。

第三章 蛹

"但我是虫，不是人，被众人羞辱，被百姓藐视"

（诗篇 22:6）

冉竹离开生活十八年的城市，就读于另一个城市的高校。四年大学结束，很少人知道冉竹的存在。冉竹申请到了新西兰一所大学硕士专业，离开生活二十二年的祖国。初到新西兰的冉竹，感觉自己好像在中国全部的学习过程中没有学过英语一样，什么都听不懂，想表达的时候，脑子里的词汇像自己做的夹生饭里的米粒一样松散着，夹生饭不能吃，应试英文不能用。各种费用支出让冉竹知道她必须尽快找份工作，确保自己能生存下来，能完成学业，能长远逃离开那永难抹去的耻辱苦难，冉竹不知道的是更多的苦难正在集结成乌云，大雨将至。

　　下课后的冉竹一路奔跑到车站，下一班要等半小时，冉竹正在试用期，迟到意味着失去好不容易得到的工作。面试那天冉竹很紧张，怕听不懂也讲不明，很幸运只有一个酒店宴会部门管工，直接带着求职者们去到厨房示范。酒店的厨房很开阔，烹饪区域以外还有很多其他食物准备区域，全是成排包着不锈钢的食物处理台，管工在一处摆着好些大椭圆形托盘的台子前停下，先放三个大的餐碟在托盘上，然后分别盖上不锈钢盖，然后同样方式加上第二和第三层。然后半蹲下把托盘连同上面的九份餐放在肩膀上，接下来就需要肩、腰，腿同时发力，扛起托盘走向宴会大厅。宴会大厅里四周摆放着一些打开了的折叠支架，每两个支架成一组，一个空着，另一个上面放着空的相同样式的大椭圆形托盘，走到空着的那个支架前，再次半蹲下把托盘转移到支架上放稳就可以开始。首先揭开最上层三个餐盖放到旁边空的托盘上，接着将三个餐碟，一只手的拇指、食指和中指固定住第一个，然后以拇指背、无名指和小拇指构成一个三角形支点，放第二个在上面，另一只手端第三个，接下到就可以走到餐桌旁依次放到客人面前，九份餐用完再回到厨房扛另外九份，直到自己负责的客人都有食物，每个服务生负责四或五桌，每桌十人左右，通常分别有前餐，正餐和甜点，每道餐客人吃完需要立刻收走餐碟和餐具，以便服务下一道餐，收的餐盘放在已经空了的托盘上，餐具放进餐盖里。然后整托盘扛回厨房的洗碗间，接着继续扛下一道餐。周而复始，直到宴会结束，清理水杯和咖啡杯，重新铺上桌布，准备好第二天的宴会所需。

求职者们开始演示新学到的工作程序，第一个站起来的时候，因为托盘有些倾斜导致最上层的三个餐碟连同餐盖一起摔倒地上，瓷器的破碎声，金属盖的撞击声震耳欲聋，其他求职者都紧张起来，也分外谨慎起来，轮到冉竹，她拼尽全力也没办法扛起那个对于她如同五指山的托盘。管工说很抱歉，我们最低要求是能扛九份餐，现在只是空盘子你都扛不了，加上食物后就更不用说了。冉竹结结巴巴地说自己很需要这份工作以便能完成学业，请管工能给一个工作机会，自己一定努力锻炼身体，保证尽快能扛起来。或许同样是女性的缘故，管工看着瘦弱的冉竹心生怜悯，讲好三个月试用期结束前必须达标。冉竹又是激动又是感激，于是给了管工一个大大的拥抱，管工意味深长地笑了笑。

　　酒店坐落在海边，生意很好，作为新人的冉竹也幸运得到足够的工作时间。酒店厨房每次都会多准备很多餐以备不时之需，所以宴会结束后保温柜里多余的食物就给员工吃，美食和奔跑，加上持续工作训练，逐渐强壮起来的冉竹很快就成功扛起了九份餐，也扛起了生活的沉重。圣诞新年购物狂欢后的人们没有了消费，酒店会利用这个生意萧条的空隙举办年庆，为感谢过去的一年里员工们辛勤的工作。为了让员工能尽情吃喝，不必担心酒后驾车回家发生交通事故，酒店当晚还为员工提供免费客房。宴会的时候管工和冉竹坐在同一桌，自从管工当初破格录用了冉竹，冉竹一直很感激她，所以有空的时候冉竹会请她吃饭，管工也会邀请冉竹一起看电影、去远足、听音乐会、和游泳。太阳早早跳出了海平面，冉竹被窗帘缝隙透进来的光线照醒。冉竹努力回忆着这是什么地方，脑袋很重，身体很重，冉竹试着爬起来，但被子一边牢固地塞在床垫下，另外一边像被重物压着，冉竹的眼睛慢慢适应了房间的光线，转头想看看是什么压着被子，一个一丝不挂躺在被子上的身体惊得冉竹立刻清醒了，才发现自己也是一丝不挂。冉竹的心快提到嗓子眼了，脑子里努力搜寻着试图想起发生了什么事。旁边的身体动了动，管工那熟悉的声音让冉竹坠入了深渊。管工翻身钻进被子贴了过来，或许在被子外很久了，管工的身体很凉，冉竹不禁打了个寒战。管工揉了揉冉竹的头发问她睡得好不好？饿不饿？待会儿要不要先去游泳回来再计划其他的项目？冉竹僵直得躺着一动不动，冉竹怨恨自己前一晚在年庆期间喝太多酒。冉竹记起自己面试那一天，管工说自己没能达到录用的最低要求，冉竹希望管工给自己一个机会，冉竹希望管工当初没有答应。冉竹不知道自己是怎么拿着衣服在海滩上不停地跑着，清晨的日光从高天临到她脸上，冉竹哭得撕心裂肺。

　　冉竹辞了工作，租了新住处，房东是一位单亲妈妈，九岁的女儿患有自闭症。房东说之前家里太安静，安静到令人窒息，她很开心冉竹搬来住，让她每天能睡得安心。这并没有让冉竹每天带着开心能睡得安心。冉竹整夜整夜地失眠，脑袋很重，身体很重，让她无法呼吸。冉竹停止做任何事情，不打扫房间，不整理物品，不洗衣服，不洗澡，她的生活混乱不堪，她身上的气味令人作呕，冉竹把自己关在房间里不吃不喝。房东因为习惯自闭症女儿的日常，冉竹又是新搬进来，所以并不觉得冉竹的异常。直到有一天房东发现躺在厕所地上的冉竹没了反应，才惊慌失措地叫了救护车来。在医院醒来的冉竹手臂上插着针头，输入的液体很凉，冉竹不禁打了个寒颤。冉竹问来查房的医生自己什么时候可以离开医院，医生说冉竹绝食导致酮中毒需要治疗。

房东带来煮好的鸡汤给冉竹，冉竹很抱歉平白给她添这么大的麻烦，房东安慰冉竹不要多虑，既然住在一个屋檐下，就是家人，如果病的是她，冉竹一定会做同样的事情。冉竹抱着这一份暖融融，哭得泣不成声。

政府的一位社工来探访，告诉冉竹安心治疗，她会帮助冉竹申请残疾福利。第二天来了另一位社工，询问冉竹为什么要自杀？如果真的想结束生命，为什么要在有人能发现的地方？冉竹没有回答。其实她想告诉社工笑傲的死因，但她什么也没有说。自杀必须要成为尸体，一旦活过来，可能会被取消正常生活的权力，甚至会被关进精神病院。

冉竹被转去了精神病专区，是位于医院北侧一幢独立的楼。整栋楼朝外的窗户全部安装着严密的钢筋护栏，工作人员需用门禁卡才可以出入。来访者需要提起预约，到了预约时间，需有护理人员通过音频视频闸机系统授权才能进出。

精神病区很少有探访者。冉竹记得之前去癌症中心探望鼻咽癌的师母时，各个病房都满了探访者。统计数据显示，癌症死亡人数占世界死亡人口的 16.7%，精神病死亡人数占全世界死亡人口的 14.3%， 癌症病人和精神病人及其家属都承受着巨大的痛苦，但前者受到的社会关注程度，支持力度，同情指数……仅次于公众人物；然而后者却被世人厌弃，包括医护人员。

精神病人彼此不交流，每一个人都仿佛裹在自己的茧房里，的确这世界和其上的是危险的。为了打发时间冉竹开始观察她所能看见的。病人们一进去，会被没收所有物品，穿医院提供的病服和袜子，不许穿鞋。病人会有一位主治医生和一位心理医生，主治医生通常会有两个实习医生作为助理，实习医生在主治医生见病人前，先和病人聊天三十分钟，记录下所有细节，之后会给病人预定好见主治医生的时间。主治医生带着实习医生一起见病人的时间在十五到三十分钟范围内，依照病情而定，主治医生一边看实习医生的记录同时问病人一些问题。如果是刚进来的病人，主治医生会把为病人开的处方交给实习医生，如果是长住病人，主治医生会依照治疗结果调整用药和用量。实习医生会把病人的用药和用量信息传递给护理人员，护理人员会按时分发药和水给病人，必须确保病人完全吞咽下药物。护理人员通常工作四天休息四天，每天十二小时，每四小时休息十五分钟，外加三十分钟用餐时间。夜班的护理人员比白天工作者心情差一些，晚上通常每两小时查房一次，用刺眼的手电光扫描病人周身，尤其不放过眼睛。冉竹很理解护理人员，他们不能睡觉，病人怎么可以。有时候当班护理人员有紧急事情不能上班，尤其是夜班，就会有顶替护理人员来，因为不是正式员工，所以略微有些恣意妄为，有几次晚上查房，冉竹都被替补护工质问为什么自杀，为什么浪费公共资源。冉竹无言以对，因为冉竹能确信这些人并不是真的希望听精神病患者的答案，更不希望病人开口打断他们的情绪宣泄。病人们通常很沉默，因为晚上不能睡安稳，所以白天除了吃饭和吃药，其他时间多数人都在睡。也有不睡的，有的在走廊上来回踱步；有的在餐厅不停给电视换台；有的站在图书室面对文字呐呐自语；有的不停去找护理人员要食物的或是反复强调自己身体很不适；有请求打电话让家人来探望自己的，如果遇到个别情绪失控的病人，会被保安人员控制住，关在另外一处独立隔间，虽然精神病区的病人没有自由，但是关禁闭触发了渴望自由的灵魂，呐喊响彻整栋建筑。作为观察者，冉竹开始是为了消磨时间，后来是为了不浪费时间，冉竹希望自己不被白白消耗在那里。

出院那天，房东来接冉竹，冉竹终于重新穿上了鞋，感觉有根有基。成为观察者，冉竹一进到这个自己居住的地方，第一次细细打量了一遍。整体感觉简单干净，东西摆放整齐有序，最显眼的地方有一幅字："基督是我家之主。"对于一直拼劲全力争取自己做主却落得劳苦愁烦的冉竹，非常想看看一个不自己做主，生活、动作、存留都在乎基督的人的结局如何。

冉竹在一家电池和能源设备设计和制造企业产品开发部门任职，这是一家美国独资经营的电池技术公司，采用最先进的技术和创新工艺制造电池。冉竹所在的产品开发部门负责热电池技术的研发工作，主要用于需要一次性电源的军事和航天应用。冉竹公司制造并开发的热电池因其免维护、长寿命和高功率特性，能够在极端温度范围和气候条件下运行，成了广泛应用于各种军事领域领先的热电池制造商，包括导弹、弹药、鱼雷、弹射座椅、制导系统、声纳浮标和运载火箭。因为电池制作过程中不能有任何污染，并且温度和湿度都必须控制在要求的范围之内，所以工作间内除了设备、材料和特定的人员外不许有任何其他物品。每个工作间出入都设置空气阻隔间，员工从第一道门进入阻隔间内，需穿上已经消毒过的白大褂，就是医院医生穿的那种；带上帽子，和糕点师同款；口罩、手套和鞋套也都带好以后，才可以打开第二道门进入工作间。冉竹的工作除了研发，还需要在各个工作间测试生产出来的不同种类电池的各项指标是否达到标准。午餐休息的半小时，冉竹出和入工作间的脱和穿全套装备就用掉了十分钟，洗手间又十分钟，剩下十分钟不够吃饭，所以冉竹省略掉午饭。公司员工是来自各个国家的移民，新西兰本地人主要从事政府机构类型的工作，或者是本地一些大公司，很少就职于外国公司，也少见从事体力或者技术工作，如果有在此类行业工作的，多数也是在管理层。移民的最大问题是很难融入本地圈子，所以只好固守着自己的语言、文化和意识形态。尤其是来自经济落后，文化匮乏，信息封闭，政治压抑……的国家的移民，通常会表现出一种对其他国家移民的非理性仇视，虽然大多数人掩饰着，但有导火索，冲突就可能爆发。更危险的是这些人一旦有了权力，无论权力大小都会是被管理者的一场灾难，或许因为有些移民国家的人民在本国需要屈从于权力，所以他们会极度渴望权力，一旦当权很大比例会滥用权力，并天真地以为其他人应该像他们曾经屈从于权力一样听从于他们，当遇到不惟命是从者的时候，他们自卑的自尊心就会被伤害到。没有加入午餐行列的冉竹错过了重要的社交场合，没有参与同事间的聊天以及是是非非的冉竹形同异类，加上冉竹声明自己生活、动作、存留都是为蒙主的喜悦，不是要讨人的喜欢；再加上冉竹坚持不接中新冠疫苗，所有这些都是引发战争爆发的诱因。因为省略掉午餐，所以冉竹通常会比其他人早些进入工作间，避免了午餐结束后各个工作间都需要排队依次进入的麻烦。一位和冉竹同时间入职的员工升职成为小组长当天，午餐结束回来的她看见已经在里面的冉竹，她询问冉竹在这里干什么，但是因为员工们的进入后引发工作间的温湿度变化，所以控温湿度设备立刻开始启动，噪音盖过了小组长从口罩后传出的声音，加上冉竹带着一只耳机听歌，所以完全没听到小组长的询问。小自尊受到了大伤害的小组长跑去向经理投诉，经理来发现了冉竹带着耳机，于是要求工作期间不允许再带，冉竹对此很不以为然，这激怒了喜欢鸡毛当令箭的经理，另外冉竹没有接种新冠疫苗，数罪并罚，经理向总部汇报后，得到公司总人事部批准辞退了冉竹。

第四章 破茧而出

"所以，我们藉着洗礼归入死，和祂一同埋葬，原是叫我们一举一动有新生的样式，像基督藉着父的荣耀从死里复活一样"

（罗马书 6:4）

冉景明死于圣诞佳节普世欢腾之日，死亡常常唤起人类的思考，冉竹开始认真思考继续原有的生活轨迹，还是开始一种全新的方式。前者的结局就是死，后者引发了作为观察者的冉竹的好奇，她决定探索个究竟。冉竹开始厄瓜多尔的短宣之旅，接待的家庭旅馆一家人非常热情，女主人退休前是当地学校的英文老师，所以是主要经营者，丈夫只讲西班牙语，承担着客房的维护工作，他们有个儿子是导游，空闲的时候会带着冉竹他们到处看看。在赤道线上，冉竹成功立起了一个鸡蛋，并获得了赤道蛋证书，冉竹左右两脚之间标记着"0"、

"0"、"0"维度赤道标志，左脚南半球的水槽下水漩涡顺时针旋转，右脚北半球的水槽下水漩涡逆时针旋转。冉竹思想着人在世上的境况，例如遇到顺或逆境，其实是基于自己行事为人，一念之间左右摇摆，或顺着心中的纯正慈怜谦卑，行在光明路上，凡事顺利；或逆着心里的良善任意妄为，活在幽暗之地，自招祸患。在钦博拉索山，这个地球表面上离地心最远之处，冉竹第一次离自己的心很近，冉竹之前从没有真正地关心过心，和心说说话，了解一下心的感受，甚至任由心挨饿受冻，感恩的是冉竹终于开始给心供应那生命的粮，让心在主的道上受了教训，心里火热。冉竹最热爱赤道之国有各式各样色彩斑斓的蝴蝶，蝴蝶也很钟爱冉竹，经常静静地停在冉竹头发上，衣服上，展开的手臂上，和那本翻开的圣经上，上面写着："若有人在基督里，他就是新造的人，旧事已过，都变成新的了"（哥林多后书5:17）。冉竹思想着人在地上的生命，好像包在茧里的蛹，死亡如同破茧而出时消失了的蛹，其实生命没有消失，而是变成新的更美的生命。

杜芷死于新冠疫情肆虐全球之时。灾难常常显露人类的本性。被公司辞退的冉竹没有疫苗接种卡就拿不到任何政府补贴。各种费用支出让冉竹知道她必须尽快找份工作，确保自己能生存下来，能验证信心，能长久忍耐得那永不衰残的荣耀冠冕，冉竹不知道的是更多的试炼正在集结成队伍，争战将至。

疫情让很多人害怕染上病毒而不愿意外出工作，冉竹了解到很多建筑工地急需劳动工人，因为是在户外工作，所以不过度要求疫苗接种卡。冉竹投去简历给几家建筑公司后，很快几家公司纷纷抛来橄榄枝给冉竹，冉竹茅塞顿开，一个崭新的计划在冉竹思想里成型。冉竹迅速联络了自己认识的几个新移民新西兰碰巧遭遇疫情找不到工作的同胞，并请他们分别联系认识的同样状况的人，很快冉竹有了一个 20 多人的队伍。冉竹的公司和多家建筑总承包商都有签约。建筑公司按人均 32 元每小时支付给冉竹公司，冉竹支付自己工人 18 元每小时。随着疫情结束，经济开始复苏，人员流动加剧，地产行业最先嗅到商机，纷纷开始新开发项目，于是冉竹公司的生意越来越好。然而"骄傲在败坏以先；狂心在跌倒之前"（箴言书 16:18）。 混得风生水起的冉竹日渐自夸，狂傲。忘记神话语的提醒--- "使你与人不同

的是谁呢？你有什么不是领受的呢？若是领受的，为何自夸，仿佛不是领受的呢？"（哥林多前书 4:7）

冉竹的公司属于建筑劳务分包商性质。冉竹除了提供劳务人员，安排工作事项，还需要参加建筑总承包商日常例行会议，以了解每天的工地情况，各个分包商之间所需的协调合作，最重要的就是安全问题，有时各分包商头目需要强制参加安全培训，以便再培训自己的人员。那一年的天气很异常，那一天的日常例行会议气氛很异常，总承包商的安全主管简单叙述了一下前一天工地有人员坠楼身亡的事，没有讲述坠楼原因，只是要求各分包商头目必须参加当天的心理健康急救培训。参加完心理健康急救培训的冉竹需要吹吹风。冉竹站在 52 楼顶层，不知道为什么冉竹突然记起电影追捕里的台词："杜丘，你看，多么蓝的天，走过去，你可以融化在蓝天里，一直走不要朝两边看，明白吗？杜丘，快，去吧！"冉竹莫名其妙地笑出了声，在空旷的楼层回响成一种恐怖的声音，惊了冉竹一身冷汗。风吹得声音越来越大，冉竹的脑袋开始嗡嗡作响，继而轰鸣到震耳欲聋。冉竹不记得自己怎样走过去融化在蓝天里，只记得身体坠落的时候，仿佛有一种巨大的力量托住了她，接着有种沉闷的疼痛席卷全身，然后冉竹没了知觉。

一男一女两位警察轮班一直在医院直到冉竹醒来，他们很详细询问和记录冉竹的信息，男警察告诉冉竹他的父母是沈阳人，看到父母那一代人在异国文化冲击下的挣扎，他知道作为第一代移民的辛酸。所以当他看见冉竹时特别心酸，还告诉冉竹一些作为警察不需要讲的详情---因为楼层高风很大，冉竹又比较瘦小，从 52 楼坠落的她被大风吹着在平移中下坠落在 47 层露台上，露台边缘林立的预埋钢筋之中因为有一根的裸露钢筋头上缺失了钢筋安全保护帽，导致钢筋扎入冉竹的腹部。高层坠楼的人之中，冉竹这样的结果很罕见，他真心希望大难不死的冉竹以后能好好生活。奇迹常常提醒人类的渺小。冉竹深知若不是创造宇宙和其中万物的神，用大能和伸出来的膀臂保护她，她早已归回尘土了。

医生来例行检查，他异常和蔼可亲地询问冉竹感觉怎样？冉竹想坐起来向医生了解一下伤势，腹部剧烈的疼痛让冉竹大大蜷曲，大汗淋漓。医生告诉冉竹她真的很幸运，扎入腹部的钢筋并没有伤到冉竹的肠道，所以不需要进行手术清理腹腔，不过肝脏有轻微受损，好在肝脏有很强的再生能力。冉竹没有吃护士拿给她的止疼药，身体的剧痛能分散心里的伤痛，因为冉竹知道自己的过犯，得罪了赐给她生命的神，没有神的同在，冉竹的世界荒废凄凉，冉竹的内心空虚荒凉。冉竹的钱财不能救她，冉竹知道这事临到她是因她骄傲，自夸自大。她稍微活动一下就头晕气喘，因为失血过多，护士每天测完冉竹的血压，都要求她静卧以防止昏倒，冉竹每次的验血结果也遍布着红色警示标志，冉竹终日满身疼痛，心中悲哀，想着自己再也不可能恢复成原来的状态了。身心俱疲的冉竹打开很久没有读的圣经，恰好是约翰一书 2:15-17 "不要爱世界和世界上的事。人若爱世界，爱父的心就不在他里面了。因为，凡世界上的事，就像肉体的情欲、眼目的情欲，并今生的骄傲，都不是从父来的，乃是从世界来的。这世界和其上的情欲都要过去，惟独遵行神旨意的，是永远常存。" 冉竹像个犯了错的孩子在严厉慈爱的父亲面前："神啊，求你按你的慈爱怜恤我！按你丰盛的慈悲涂抹我的过犯！……不要丢弃我，使我离开你的面；不要从我收回你的圣灵……神啊，忧伤痛悔的心，你必不轻看"（诗篇

51:1，11，17b）。"求你宽容我，使我在去而不返之先可以力量复原"（诗篇 39:13）。

奇迹般存活下来的冉竹，又奇迹般的痊愈了。鸟儿们的歌唱，阳光在树间的穿梭，植物们尽情吸着二氧化碳，释放出的氧气让晨跑中的冉竹心旷神怡。冉竹之所以决定去神学院装备自己，为要常常提醒自己，救主耶稣基督，祂本有神的形象，却为她以及众人的罪能得以赦免，祂舍自己作万人的赎价，道成了肉身，成为人的样式，藉着祂在十字架上所流的血成就了和平，叫万有都与神和好了，神照自己的大怜悯，藉耶稣基督从死里复活，使那些已信神的人得以重生，有活泼的盼望，脱离罪和死亡的辖制。为了让更多人听到这宝贵的真理，活成神起初所造的人本该有的样式：敬畏神，远离恶事；尊重生命，照着神形象被造的人需要停止彼此伤害；学会感恩和分享，逃避一切的怨恨、假善、诡诈、邪恶、贪婪、恶毒、嫉妒、争竞……，存怜悯、恩慈、谦虚、温柔、忍耐的心真诚待人。

神学院冉竹认真在神的话语上装备自己，随时随刻听神差遣，毕业了的冉竹开启了宣教之旅，透过舷窗冉竹看到自己在云层之上，如鹰展翅上腾。

结　语

"我思想我所行的道，就转步归向你的法度"

（诗篇　119:59）

　　中国移民群体，心里始终自定义为寄居者，没有归属感，也找不到文化认同感，好像旧约里的以色列人。纵使神应许赐给他们流奶与蜜之地，他们却在旷野飘流无定。然而持守信仰的人们承认自己在世上是客旅，是寄居的。然而，至高者的圣民，必要丰丰富富地得以进入我们主，救主耶稣基督永远的国，作祂的子民，直到永远。

羽化

Chapter 1   Larva

"The cords of death encompassed me; the torrents of destruction assailed me. The cords of Sheol entangled me; the snares of death confronted me"

(Psalm 18:4–5)

Ran Zhu was awakened by her sister's startled cry. Soon, the yard filled with hurried footsteps mixed with sobbing, and her little heart pounded violently. She hurriedly dressed and slipped on her shoes, rushing out to find the adults already gathered in her grandmother's room, "grandma..." Ran Zhu stood bewildered, staring at her grandmother's motionless body on the bed, her throat only able to utter broken sounds. The adults would not let her approach the corpse, but she longed snuggling with grandmother as she used to, listening to her stories of the past, rubbing her face against her grandmother's cheek until her grandmother wrapped her tightly in her arms and touched her nose to hers, whispering, "My little Piggy (Piggy and Zhuzhu have the same pronunciation in Chinese) is ready for sleep". Nothing in the world felt safer than falling asleep in the warmth of grandmother's breath. Ran Zhu remembered one summer afternoon when they lay together in the courtyard, beneath the shade of the jujube tree on the old reclining chair. A flock of wild geese passed overhead in perfect V-formation, Ran Zhu asked why the geese must fly away? And grandmother told her that the geese went to find their grandmother. Clutching grandmother tightly, Ran Zhu whispered, "but you mustn't leave me like their grandmother did, if you fly away, I'll never know where to find you." Grandmother kissed her cheek and said gently, "One day, I will have to fly away too, but my little Piggy must be brave, and grow into a strong girl." With her small face pressed against grandmother's face, four lines of tears fell.

Ran Zhu's birth was an accident. Ran Jingming and Du Ruo already had four children, and with their work keeping them constantly busy, not to mention the weight of complicated social entanglements, they were often restless and worn, especially Du Ruo. Ran Zhu's grandfather was a businessman. He and grandmother had once had six children. The eldest was a daughter, Du Zhi; the youngest, Du Ruo. Between the two sisters had been four brothers, all of whom died young from smallpox. As a result, Du Zhi had to marry a man into the family to preserve the line. Being twenty-one years older than her sister, Du Zhi's eldest daughter was born the same year Du Ruo was born. The household overflowed with new life and laughter that year. Du Ruo was born beautiful in form and appearance. After the devastating loss of their four sons, her parents found comfort in her arrival, and under their adoration she grew ever more radiant, her beauty blossomed alongside a growing pride and arrogance. Because of Du Zhi bore five daughters, no sons. Then Du Ruo too was expected to find a husband willing to marry into the family. It was then that Ran Jingming, a young man who had come alone to the city where the Du family lived, hoping to carve out a life for himself. He found employment in grandfather's business.

Handsome, gentle, and intelligent, Ran Jingming was often invited to the Du household. Each time, he lingered, reluctant to leave, for he was captivated by Du Ruo. Eventually, it seemed only natural that he married into the Du family. In marriage, Du Ruo's pride and arrogance flourished all the more, fueled by her husband's adore. Witnessing his son-in-law being tortured to the point of collapse by Du Ruo, Ran Jingming's father-in-law gave him a calligraphy, "***Being and non-being produce each other; difficult and easy complete one another; long and short contrast each other; high and low depend on one another; sound and voice harmonize with each other; front and back follow one another. Such is the way of constancy.***" Though Du Ruo was imperious, Ran Jingming cherished her all his life, sufficient to prove that calligraphy came into his heart as it was working. But in later years, amidst chaos and turmoil, both the calligraphy and the family's gold and treasures vanished without a trace, the Du family gradually declined. Many years later, when Ran Zhu returned from New Zealand to visit her parents, time had already softened old grievances. She had already reconciled with her parents, and even spoke freely about many things. One day, as Ran Zhu was sharing from the Bible, particularly from 1 Corinthians, chapter 13, Ran Jingming's eyes lit with sudden clarity. "Once," he said, "your grandfather gave me a calligraphy scroll. And thinking on it now, I realize, human beings share a common wisdom, it true that God made from one man every nation of mankind over all of the earth."

To return to the matter of Ran Zhu's birth was an accident. Ran Jingming and Du Ruo already had four children, and with their work keeping them constantly busy, not to mention the weight of complicated social entanglements, they were often restless and worn, especially Du Ruo, she can no longer bear the trouble of having another child, so when Ran Jingming voiced his wish for one more, Du Ruo had firmly refused. Yet what man plans, God overrules. Du Ruo became pregnant with a fifth child,　this was hard for her to accept as she was used to getting her way at home, she poured her anger, resentment, and bitterness, and all of the negative emotions are vented on the innocent fetus, Du Ruo hoped most that this child would be a miscarriage before the due date, vanishing as though it had never existed. Born out of such cruelty, Ran Zhu was rebellious from the very beginning, even her birth defied expectations. She thrust one leg out first, so that the delivery became a desperate struggle to turn her around so her head could emerge. What appeared was a translucent, purplish infant that terrified everyone present. Had her eldest cousin not been there, already an experienced obstetrician and head of her department, Ran Zhu might have been discarded as a monstrosity. Her eldest cousin recounted how unruly her birth had been: the umbilical cord wrapped around her neck during rotation, and the amniotic sac did not break. Any one of these complications could have suffocated her. But with her eldest cousin quick action to cut the cord, tearing the sac, and holding her upside down while striking her until at last a cry rang out, only then did Ran Zhu live. And yet, Ran Zhu carried no gratitude for this rescue. She loathed her own arrival into the world. She believed her mother must have felt the same, for Du Ruo had despised the very fact of carrying her. Beyond the unwanted pregnancy, Du Ruo resented the agony of that difficult labor, the suffering she had never endured before. Du Ruo feared the curses and bitterness she had during pregnancy had taken root, that this child had come to exact revenge. Ran Zhu had resentment to Du Ruo, perhaps it stemmed from the womb, though she could not know what she had experienced there, but that resentment reached its height one day during a quarrel between her parents. Ran Jingming listed Du Ruo's many faults, recalled how when Ran Zhu was small, Du Ruo often traveled for work, gone for days at a time. During those absences, little Ran Zhu would wrap herself in her mother's quilted jacket, stand at the front gate, and refuse food or drink. She would not step back inside, waiting stubbornly like a little mule until she collapsed from exhaustion, only then could Ran Jingming scoop her up and carry her back into the house. Du Ruo's heart softened when she heard this story. She began, for the first time, to treat Ran Zhu with some warmth. Years later, when Ran Zhu left for a faraway land, her mother even pressed that quilted jacket as a keepsake. But Ran Zhu absolutely did not believe this story, it was a humiliation to her strong self, therefore, Ran Zhu firmly believed her father had made it up, and she did not need a mother at all, just as Ran Zhu believed her mother did not need her either. This was why, from the time she could remember, Ran Zhu clung so closely to her grandmother. She truly loved her grandmother, for in her small world, grandmother is the only one who does not cherishes nothing but her little Piggy. Even though Ran Zhu's second old and third old brother often took her along when they went out to play, in those days, boys' games were little harsh and left them often came home bruised up and dirty. Hoping for home to be a safe harbor, they instead returned to storms even fiercer. Ran Zhu never thought her brothers took her along out of love, but only to share the blame when they returned home bruised up and dirty. Yet as time passed, dissatisfaction in her heart faded like the scars on her skin.

Ran Zhu missed her grandmother. Whenever the wild geese flew overhead, she would lift her face toward the sky and silently beg them to take her along, because only the geese never forgot, year after year, to go in search of their grandmother. Flying so high, they must surely be able to see that better and more beautiful place where her grandmother now dwelled. Beneath the shade of the jujube tree in the courtyard, the reclining chair was often occupied by the fifth cousin, sprawled carelessly, sometimes flashing Ran Zhu a ghostly smile. After Ran Zhu's eldest aunt and uncle passed away, the other four cousins had already married and moved out, only the fifth cousin, though of marriageable age, had not yet found someone suitable, so she still lived in the same courtyard. She could sing and dance, yet disliked steady work, instead of she drifted from one performance opportunity to another. When there was no stage, she stayed home reading idle books, many filled with stories of love and lust. One summer afternoon, while the adults were at work and the children went to school, Ran Zhu was stuck at home with feverish from a cold. The fifth cousin was excited by what she had been reading and with nowhere to release her impulses, came over to the frail, feverish child lying on the bed and asked with a wicked smile, ***"Do you want to know what your parents did to bring you into this world?"*** Ran Zhu, full of disgust, answered that she had never wanted to be born at all. Suddenly the fifth cousin's mouth pressed against hers, while her hand slipped into Ran Zhu's underclothes. Terror swept through Ran Zhu's small body, on that hot midsummer afternoon, she shivered violently with cold, which only inflamed the fifth cousin's further. Twisting and pressing her weight upon her, she whispered, "Look at you, ***trembling with excitement***, you must like it." The fever, the shock, the fear, together they overwhelmed Ran

Zhu, and she fainted. When she opened her eyes again, a blinding white light made her shield them with her hand, and for one fleeting, blissful instant, she rejoiced, she thought she had died, that she had reached heaven where a holy and radiant place. But the fifth cousin's familiar voice shattered the illusion: ***"Ah, you finally woke up!"*** Ran Zhu was dragged back to hell. She tried to get up to escape, but nurses and her parents, who seemed to appear from nowhere, held her down. Struck dumb with terror, she let out a scream so piercing it felt as if it could rip open the mask of the world. According to the fifth cousin's account to the doctors and Ran Zhu's parents, the girl had collapsed in a high fever, delirious with nonsense. Fortunately, the fifth cousin had been at home and rushed her to the hospital before the fever could burn away her mind. The doctor suggested her parents to let Ran Zhu take a break from school for a while. Ran Zhu's third old brother felt sad watching her languish at home. Around that time, his classmate's cat had given birth to a litter. He brought one of the kittens back for her. Holding this furry ball, Ran Zhu sobbed uncontrollably.

The little cat was named Maoqiu. During her leave from school, Maoqiu became a warm ray in her life. When Ran Zhu eventually returned to school, she remained silent. She no longer played with classmates, nor joined her brothers in their war games with the other boys. Ran Zhu hoped to be able to fight against malice by isolating herself from all around her. Between classes, Ran Zhu would walk circles around the playground, lap after lap. More than once a stray football or some other flying object struck her, but she never stopped. One day a football slammed into her face with such force that she was thrown to the ground. Lying there, she saw many feet rushing toward her, voices clamoring, dust rising all around. She was taken to the hospital with her face badly swollen and crooked. Though her cheekbone was not fractured, but the examination revealed something else: doctors discovered her facial bones had not developed fully, her jaw angle scarcely formed. Once again she withdrew from school. Each day, she endured thirty minutes of electro-acupuncture therapy on her face at the hospital. The nurse would insert the needles, switch on the current, and tell her to call after thirty minutes, the best time for stimulating muscle activity. In the silent ward, only the hum of the machine filled the air, if Ran Zhu did not call, no one came. The quiet was so deeply, she wished she could remain there forever. Ran Zhu often drifted into sleep as the buzzing current, waking more than an hour later with her face numb. On the first day, panic seized her, and she called frantically for the nurse, fearing permanent damage, but the nurse assured her firmly it would leave no harm. From then on, she slept soundly with the buzzing current, this became the first seed of her later insomnia. Ran Zhu slept less and less at night, Awake, Ran Zhu began to write poems that she did not even understand. Her third old brother admired them and wanted to help her get them published, but Ran Zhu refused. The world and everything in it no longer related to her, her world had been shattered that summer afternoon. It was not until years later in New Zealand, on a golden autumn

Sunday afternoon, sitting on a faded wooden bench outdoors with a Bible in her lap, that she read Psalm 18. When she reached verse 16: "He sent from on high, He took me; He drew me out of many waters." and on to verse 19: "He brought me out into a broad place; He rescued me; because He delighted in me." The sunlight filtered through the leaves above, scattering across her face like flapping wings. Memories of the past flashed before her, and to her astonishment she realized her heart no longer held resistance, bitterness, no resentment. Instead it was filled with joy. Ran Zhu gave thanksgiving to God with all her heart, a radiant gladness welled up in her and rejoice overflowed, and then Ran Zhu knew that her world had been rebuilt.

Chapter 2   Pupation

"And a young man named Eutyhus, setting at the window, sank into a deep sleep as Paul talked still longer. And being overcome by sleep, he fell down from the third story and was taken up dead"

(Acts 20:9)

Maoqiu was dead. Its little body had been crushed by a heavy object. Ran Zhu hoped desperately that Maoqiu had not suffered any broken bones, whole in its frame, full of strength, joyfully running free at that better and more beautiful place where Maoqiu now dwelled. Quietly, she buried Maoqiu, without shedding a single tear. The fifth cousin finally married, and Ran Zhu attended the wedding in silence, showing no trace of emotion. Ran Zhu finally was no longer afraid to go running by herself early in the mornings. At dawn, when it was still dim and cool, with few people on the road, Ran Zhu reached a corner and saw a cardboard box by the roadside, it seemed to be moving, leaning closer, she discovered inside a tiny white creature, like a miniature piggy, looking around for someone to ask,

Ran Zhu spotted an old man jogging past and quickly ran after him, begging him to come take a look, the old man, kind at heart, followed her back to the box. Ran Zhu asked whether it was a piggy or a puppy, because it looked so much like a piggy and she certainly did not want to raise a piggy. The old man laughed until tears ran down his face and told Ran Zhu **there's no such thing as a piggy this small, it's a little puppy, should be newborn, its eyes haven't even opened, at this size, cold and hungry, it won't survive.** Ran Zhu's heart clenched. She picked up the box and declared that **little puppy will survive, and must survive.** Ran Zhu ran home with little puppy, at that time, her second old brother, newly graduated from university and still at home preparing for his new job, was the only one she could turn to. With school starting soon, Ran Zhu hurriedly woke him up, briefly explained the discovery, and stressed that the urgent question was how to keep the little puppy alive. Being older and more educated, he quickly thought of a baby bottle left at home by their niece. He mixed milk powder, tested the temperature on his wrist, and gently brought the bottle to the puppy's nose, perhaps catching the milky flavor, the little puppy stumbled eagerly toward it, with brother helping, little puppy latched onto the nipple, but before they could contain their joy, the tiny body began coughing, choking, trembling all over, Ran Zhu broke down, grabbed her schoolbag, and fled the house in a frenzy. When Ran Zhu returned after school, she saw her brother playing with the little puppy who staggered clumsily across the table. Brother told Ran Zhu that he had found a syringe in the room their eldest cousin's used to live in, sterilized it, and used it to feed milk to the little puppy, brother also told her that **little puppy ate constantly and whenever he stopped to feed, then little puppy nudges him with the little nose, brother jokingly that no wonder Ran Zhu thought little puppy was a little piggy, honestly, they are no difference.** For the first time in a long while, a smile broke across Ran Zhu's face. Also, Ran Zhu was deeply grateful that her brother never mentioned again the way she had stormed out that morning like someone possessed. In fact, she wanted to tell her brother that horrible thing which had once happened to her, but she said nothing. The truth had to remain a secret. If ever it were spoken aloud, one might lose the right to live a "normal" life, perhaps even be confined to a mental hospital.

Xiao'ao was the name of Ran Zhu's puppy, from the moment he arrived, he brought endless joy into Ran Zhu' days. Every day after school, Xiao'ao would rush up to her with boundless enthusiasm, clinging tightly and refusing to let go, at first, Xiao'ao could only wrap his little paws around her shins, but as time passed, Xiao'ao grew taller while Ran Zhu's own growth slowed, their encounters became full embraces. By then Xiao'ao grew heavier than

Ran Zhu, so before he rushed at her, she always had to brace herself in a firm stance, lest she be knocked flat on her back. Often, before she even reached the gate of the courtyard, she could hear the rushing sound of Xiao'ao running close to gate. Just before pushing the gate open, Ran Zhu would gain a firm foothold, and the moment the door swung open, Xiao'ao would already leap forward, his forelegs spread wide, throwing himself into her arms with a great hug. Rainy days became a special challenge, because what awaited Ran Zhu was Xiao'ao' enthusiastic, mud-soaked embrace and he never failed to leave his mark all over her clothes. To preserve the ritual of their reunion, Ran Zhu switched from using an umbrella to wearing a raincoat. After Xiao'ao' death, Ran Zhu never again carried an umbrella or wore a raincoat on rainy days, it became her private way of remembering Xiao'ao.

Ran Jingming and Du Ruo had disliked previous cat, Maoqiu, and they disliked Xiao'ao just as much, they strictly required that Ran Zhu could only feed her pets with whatever food was left after the whole family had finished their meals. Back earlier days when Maoqiu was alive, Ran Zhu often went to the market on weekends to ask fishmongers for tiny unsellable fish to feed Maoqiu, she always felt a pang of guilt for those little fish that never had the chance to grow up. As for Xiao'ao, since he had been picked up by Ran Zhu right after birth with eyes still closed. Every day after school, Ran Zhu would bring Xiao'ao to her desk, do her homework while playing with him. In theory, being blind should have made him cautious, but Xiao'ao never followed the rules. He wobbled and stumbled recklessly, often heading straight for the edge of the desk, each time, Ran Zhu to snatch him back from landing, each near fall left her breaking out in a cold sweat and heart hammering, so Ran Zhu moved her meals to the desk as which only deepened Ran Jingming and Du Ruo dislike of Xiao'ao escalated into boredom. More than once, while they were eating, they suddenly erupted in anger, especially Du Ruo who would shout to Ran Zhu, "sit back to the dining table right now!" In those moments, Ran Zhu would shovel food into her mouth as quickly as she could, then carry her empty bowl to the kitchen, and as she passed the dining table, she could feel four cold eyes fixed on her, their chill sinking into her spine. Ran Zhu's speed eating came from Du Ruo always corrected the way she held chopsticks, so that Ran Zhu refused to use chopsticks at all, eating only with a spoon, only then did that smokeless war finally come to an end.

When Xiao'ao was a little over ten days old, one mealtime Du Ruo once again erupted, shouting at Ran Zhu. She hurriedly finished her food, carried her empty bowl to the kitchen, and when she returned to her room, Xiao'ao had already fallen from the desk to the floor. Usually, Ran Zhu always placed him safely back in his nest before stepping away. Panicked, she called out for her brother, terrified that Xiao'ao might suffer lasting harm from fallen, brother reassured her firmly that it would not. Yet his words did not ease her guilt, every night she lay awake with unease, this became the second seed of her later insomnia.

From then on, Ran Zhu' sleep grew increasingly restless, broken by repeated waking up to check whether Xiao'ao was still breathing. Though Xiao'ao survived unharmed, Ran Zhu began to notice that he seemed sluggish, even dull, and more than two weeks had passed without his eyes opening. The second old brother comforted her not to worry because Xiao'ao has always been a little slow and silly one and the only advantage was edible, also it's just been over half a month, maybe puppies only open their eyes around a full month. From then on, Ran Zhu constantly worried something might happen to Xiao'ao, she would run all the way home every day after school. Her running drew the attention of the sports teacher who suggested to Ran Zhu's head teacher to let Ran Zhu join the school track team. Ran Zhu refused, but the head teacher registered her name without asking and enrolled her in every school sports competition. Ran Zhu knew that she had no strength to fight authority, so she competed in the games each time, no one could match her speed except the trained athletes team. For the medals she won, her head teacher was satisfied with her. One day, rushing home, Ran Zhu found Xiao'ao somehow looked different, though she could not name it, but something had changed. Ran Zhu called her brother and he exclaimed joyfully, "Xiao'ao has opened his eyes!"Only then did Ran Zhu realize that Xiao'ao was staring at her with two round, shining, jet black eyes. Overwhelmed, she burst into tears of joy. After Xiao'ao with sight, Ran Zhu no longer had to race home each day after school. The sighted Xiao'ao shadowed her every step, never leaving her side, because of this, Ran

Jingming and Du Ruo's dislike of Xiao'ao deepened into hatred. To avoid conflict, Ran Zhu spent nearly all her time in her room. One day at dinner, she noticed Xiao'ao staring at her bowl, drooling. Suddenly, Ran Zhu realized he must be ready to eat solid food. From then on, she began a new routine: one spoonful for herself, one spoonful for Xiao'ao, with each spoonful she raised was also a way of gathering back the pieces of her once-shattered world.

Xiao'ao began to grow rapidly while Ran Zhu stopped to grew, and gradually becoming thinner and thinner. This gave her the perfect excuse to escape the school sports competition which the head teacher forced on her. She told Ran Jingming and Du Ruo that she needed to focus on her studies and had no energy to prepare for competitions. Seeing her becoming thinner and thinner, Ran Jingming told her head teacher that Ran Zhu was never again to participate in the competition. For the first time, Ran Zhu felt victory while won nothing. In those years, the last year of high school meant no new lessons, only review for the university entrance exam. Students didn't need to attend school every day, so Ran Zhu had much more time to play with Xiao'ao. Ran Jingming warned her again and again not to waste time on playthings lead to loss of ambition, each time, Ran Zhu begged her father don't objectify Xiao'ao. Ran Jingming finally fed up with this. One day, Ran Zhu came home after an exam, at the courtyard gate, she heard no rushing footsteps, when she opened the door, there were no outstretched paws, no great embrace, the courtyard so quite, Ran Zhu's head began buzzing, and then roared like thunder. The second old brother started teaching at a university far from home now, so he had moved into university's staff dormitory. Ran Zhu's fingers trembling so badly she could barely dial, forced herself to press each number correctly, finally reaching her brother' school line. The ringing tone throbbed in her ear, her heart lodged in her throat, the call was picked up and the background was noisy. Ran Zhu whispered her brother's name in a trembling voice, perhaps her voice too weak, or the noisy too loud, the operator on the other end could not seem to hear her voice clearly, so shouted, "Who are you looking for?"The buzzing in her head roared louder, until deafening. Then the other end hung up the phone. Ran Zhu still clutched the telephone receiver, long after the shrill dial tone filled her ear. Ran Zhu had never been to her brother's staff dormitory. First, because the university staff dormitory did not allow noisy creatures like chickens, ducks, geese, or dogs, but couples working together at the university were permitted to build shack near by the staff dormitory, where they could raise their noisy chickens, ducks, geese, or dogs, also they could planting quiet things as vegetables, flower and so on; Second, because every weekend her brother always came home to visit their parents and play with Ran Zhu and Xiao'ao. But her brother did not come home on the weekend after Xiao'ao disappeared. Ran Zhu called the school again, but no one answered, then she realized that school closed on the weekends. Two weeks later, her brother finally came home. The moment he saw Ran Zhu, he wept. He told Ran Zhu that three weeks earlier, when he had come home, their father had ordered him to take Xiao'ao away as far as possible. He had thought to place Xiao'ao in one of his colleagues who built shack near by the staff dormitory for their dog. The idea is that Xiao'ao wasn't giving away permanently, he could bring Xiao'ao back after Ran Zhu graduated, and since he worked at the school and could visit Xiao'ao daily then report to Ran Zhu on weekends. But Xiao'ao refused to eat or drink during the time at that colleague's place, but his colleague had not paid much attention, simply added more dog food while feeding their dog, until one day, they found Xiao'ao lying motionless, breathless, and called Ran Zhu's brother in panic. Her brother told Ran Zhu when he went to see Xiao'ao each day and Xiao'ao looked up at him, eyes brimming with tears, like a child who had lost his favorite toy, this broke him daily. Ran Zhu stood stiff as stone, she hated herself for having fed Xiao'ao spoon by spoon while he growing up little by little, then cause Xiao'ao only eat this way. She remembered the very first day Xiao'ao came home, when her brother had joked that Xiao'ao ate like a piggy, Ran Zhu wished that Xiao'ao could eat abundantly like a piggy at that better and more beautiful place where he now dwelled. In the courtyard, Ran Zhu did not know how long she smashing the spoon belong to her and Xiao'ao again and again, the afterglow of the setting sun shone on her face, and she wept until her whole chest felt torn open.

Chapter 3　Pupa

"But I am a worm and not a man, scorned by mankind and despised by the people"

(Psalm 22:6)

Ran Zhu left the city where she had lived for eighteen years to attend university in another city. Four years of study passed, and by the time graduation loomed, not much people on campus even noticed her existence. Ran Zhu received admission to a master's program in New Zealand, leaving behind the homeland where she had lived for twenty-two years. Arriving in New Zealand, Ran Zhu felt as if she had never learned English during her entire study in China, barely understand what others said, unable to find words when she wanted to speak, the vocabulary in her head scattered like half cooked grains of rice in a pot, loose, unfinished, undercooked rice cannot be eaten and under examination oriented education cannot be applied. With expenses piling up, Ran Zhu knew she had to find a job quickly to survive, to finish her studies, and to escape forever from the unbearable shame and suffering of her past. What she did not know was that more sufferings were already gathering like dark clouds, the storm is coming.

Ran Zhu ran to the bus stop after class, if she missed the bus, the next one would not come for half an hour, still in her probation period at work, being late meant losing the job she had struggled so hard to get. She remembered on the day of the interview she had been so nervous, afraid she would not understand or be able to explain herself. Fortunately, only one supervisor from the hotel's banquet department was present, and she directly led the job applicants to the kitchen for a demonstration. The kitchen was vast, not only lined with stoves and ovens but filled with endless rows of stainless-steel preparation tables. The supervisor stopped at one table laid with large oval trays, she placed three large dinner plates on a tray and covered each with a stainless steel lid, then she added a second and third layer in the same way, finally, she squatted slightly, lifted the tray with all nine covered plates onto her shoulder, and explained how one must engage shoulder, waist, and legs together to hoist it and carry it into the banquet hall. Inside of banquet hall, folding stands had been arranged in pairs around the hall, one bare, the other holding an empty tray. Reaching an empty stand, the supervisor squatted, transferred the loaded tray and set it in place ready to serving. First of all, removed the top three lids, and shifted the lids onto the empty tray beside it, next, with one hand, she pinned first plate between her thumb, forefinger, and middle finger; the back of the thumb, ring finger, and little finger formed into a triangle of balance point for the second plate; her other hand carried the third, then, walked to the dining table and placed the plate front of guests, after serving nine plates, returned to the kitchen for another tray, until every guest had been served, each server was responsible for four or five tables, about ten guests per table. There were usually three courses: entrée, main, and dessert, as soon as one course was finished, the plates and cutlery had to be cleared as quickly as possible for serving the next course. Used plates were stacked onto empty trays, and utensils placed inside the lids which removed from top of plates. The full tray was then carried back to the dishwashing area, on the way back to the banquet hall, carry out the tray for next course. Over and over, until the banquet ended, afterward, clearing glasses, cups, tablecloths, and preparing for the next event.

One by one, the applicants began to demonstrate what they had just been taught. The first, nervous, tilted the tray too much and sent the top three plates and covers crashing to the floor. The shattering of porcelain and the clang of metal rang filled the kitchen. Everyone grew tense and cautious. When it was Ran Zhu's turn, she tried with all her strength but could not lift the tray that felt like a mountain pressing her down. The supervisor said, ***"I'm sorry, but our minimum requirement is to carry nine meals,*** right now, these plates are empty. Once they're loaded with food, it will only be heavier.*"* Stammering, Ran Zhu pleaded that she desperately needed the job in order to finish her studies, promising she would train her body and soon be able to lift the trays, perhaps sympathy born of being a woman herself, the supervisor looked at the frail girl with compassion and agreed that Ran Zhu had three months to meet the standard. Ran Zhu, overwhelmed with relief and gratitude, gave the supervisor a big hug, the supervisor smiled meaningfully.

The hotel stood by the sea, with business thriving. As a newcomer, Ran Zhu was fortunate to receive enough work hours. The kitchen always prepared extra meals for banquets, and what remained in the warmers at the end of the night was given to the staff, high fat and high protein foods, constant running, together with the training of daily labor, gradually strengthened Ran Zhu. Soon, she was able to shoulder the weight of nine meals and also to shoulder the weight of life. After the frenzy of Christmas and New Year shopping, when the city quieted and spending ebbed, the hotel took advantage of the lull to hold its annual celebration, thanking employees for a year of their hard work. To let staff eat and drink freely without fear of accidents from drunk driving, the hotel even offered free rooms for the night of annual celebration. During the banquet, the supervisor sat at the same table as Ran Zhu. Ever since the day her supervisor had bent the rules to give her a chance getting a job, Ran Zhu had carried deep gratitude toward her. In her free time, she would invite the supervisor to eat out, the supervisor, in turn, invited her to movies, hikes, concerts, and swimming. The next morning, sunlight spilled through the slit of the curtains waking Ran Zhu. She tried to remember where she was. Her head felt heavy, her body heavier still. Ran Zhu tried to rise, but the blanket was tucked down tightly on one side, weighted down on the other side. As her eyes adjusted, she turned her head and saw a naked body lying on top of the blanket. Ran Zhu jolted fully awake and realized with horror that she herself was also naked. Her heart leapt into her throat, her mind desperately searching for what had happened. The naked body stirred, the familiar voice of the supervisor plunged her into the abyss. The supervisor rolled over, slipped beneath the blanket, and pressed close. Her skin was cold, having been outside the covers for long, and Ran Zhu shivered. The supervisor stroked Ran Zhu's hair gently and asked if she had slept well, if she was hungry, if she wanted to swim first before planning other activities. Ran Zhu lay stiffly and frozen, she hated herself for drinking too much last night during the annual celebration. Ran Zhu remembered her first interview, when the supervisor had said she could not meet the minimum requirement, Ran Zhu wished the supervisor had never agreed. Ran Zhu could not remember how she ended up clutching her clothes and running along the beach, the early sunlight breaking over her face, and she wept until her whole chest felt torn open.

Ran Zhu quit her job and moved into a new place. The landlord was a single mother with a nine-year-old daughter who had autism. The landlord told her that before Ran Zhu moved in, the house had been too quiet, so quiet that it's breathtaking, She really happy that Ran Zhu moved in making her could finally sleep peacefully. But this did not make Ran Zhu sleeping peacefully, nights turned into insomnia, Ran Zhu awake all nights, her head heavy, her body heavier, she felt unable to breathe, she stopped doing anything no longer cleaned her room, no longer folded her clothes, no longer washed, no longer bathed, her life slipped into chaos, her body carrying a sour, disgusting. Ran Zhu locked herself in her room, refused food, refused drink. Because the landlord is accustomed to her autistic daughter's daily routines, she did not think Ran Zhu's behavior unusual since she's just moved in. Until one day, she found Ran Zhu collapsed on the bathroom floor, unresponsive. Panicked, she called an ambulance.

Ran Zhu awoke in the hospital with a needle in her arm, the fluid being infused was cold, and Ran Zhu couldn't help but shudder. She asked the doctor when she could discharge, the doctor explained that she had developed ketosis from prolonged fasting and needed treatment.

The landlord brought her hot chicken soup. Ran Zhu apologized deeply for causing her so much trouble. But the landlord comforted her not worry, since lived under the same roof, then became a family, the landlord also told Ran Zhu that if herself was sick, Ran Zhu would do the same thing. Holding this warmth bowl, Ran Zhu sobbed uncontrollably.

A government social worker came to visit and told Ran Zhu to rest assured and receive treatment, she would help Ran Zhu apply for disability benefits. But the following day, a different social worker came to visit and asked Ran Zhu why she had tried to kill herself, and if *she truly*

wanted to end her life, why choose a place where she could be discovered. Ran Zhu did not respond. In fact, she wanted to tell the social worker the cause of Xiao'ao' death, but she said nothing. To attempt suicide must end in a corpse, if one survived, one might lose the right to live a "normal" life, perhaps even be confined to a mental hospital.

Ran Zhu was transferred to the psychiatric department, a separate building on the north side of the hospital. Every window facing outside was fitted with heavy iron bars. Staff could enter and exit only with integrated circuit card. Visitors required advance appointments, and at the appointed time, they could only pass if the staff at the audio-video checkpoint granted access.

There were very few visitors to the psychiatric department. Ran Zhu remembered that when she went to the Cancer Centre to visit professor's wife who had nasopharyngeal cancer, each of the ward were filled with visitors. Statistics showed that cancer accounted for 16.7% of global deaths, while mental illness accounted for 14.3%. Both cancer patients, mental patients and their families suffer tremendously. But the former had received social attention, support, and sympathy index… second only to that given to public figures; however, the latter was despised by people, including many medical staff.

In the psychiatric department, patients rarely spoke; each one seemed wrapped in their own cocoon, for indeed, the world and everything in it were dangerous. To kill the time, Ran Zhu began observing everything she could see. When a new patient arrived, patients' belongings were confiscated, they were given hospital-issued uniforms and socks; no shoes were allowed. Patients would have an attending psychiatrist and a psychologist, the attending psychiatrist usually followed by two interns as assistants. Each patient was first seen by two interns who would chat with patient for thirty minutes, recording every detail, the patient would then be given a scheduled appointment with the attending psychiatrist. The attending psychiatrist and the interns visited to the patient were between fifteen and thirty minutes, depending on the severity of the case, the attending psychiatrist asked the patient questions while reviewing the records from the interns. For new patients, the attending psychiatrist would pass the prescriptions which written for the patient to the interns, for long-term patients, the prescriptions would be adjusted according to treatment results. The interns then would pass the patient's prescription details to the nursing staff who distributed the medicine and water at scheduled times, ensuring every pill that patient swallowed completely. The nurses usually worked four days on, four days off, twelve hours per shift with a fifteen-minute break every four hours and thirty minutes for meals, nurses on the night shift were in a bad mood, at night they checked each room every two hours, shining sharp beams of flashlight to scan the patient's body, especially the eyes. Ran Zhu understood: the nurses could not sleep, so how could the patients? Sometimes the regular staff could not work their shift, especially night shift, the casual workers were called, these temporary replacement workers could be a little bit acting arbitrarily, a few times during night checks, temporary replacement workers questioned Ran Zhu Why the suicide occurred, why wasted public resources? Ran Zhu had no reply, because Ran Zhu was sure that these workers did not really want to hear the answers of psychopaths, also they did not want patients to interrupt their emotional outbursts. Most patients remained silent, because nights were restless, therefore, except for eating and taking medicines during the day, most patients spend the rest of the time sleeping. A few stayed awake: some paced up and down in the hallway; some sat in the dining room flipping the television channels endlessly; some muttered to oneself in front of the books in the library; some constantly asked the nurses for food or repeatedly declared that they were very unwell; some asked the nurses to call their family to pick them up, if encountered patients who lost control of their emotions, security staffs restrained them and locked them into a separate isolation room, although patients in the psychiatric department had no freedom, but being locked up triggered their souls longing for freedom, shouts echoed throughout the entire building. As an observer, Ran Zhu at first to kill the time, later it became her way not to waste the time. Ran Zhu hoped that she would not be consumed in vain within those walls.

On the discharge day, the landlord came to pick up Ran Zhu, and she finally put her shoes back on and felt being rooted and grounded again. Became an observer, as soon as Ran Zhu entered the place where she lived, Ran

Zhu scanned it carefully for the first time. The overall feeling was simple and clean, everything arranged neatly and in order. On the most conspicuous wall hung a calligraphy: **"Christ is the head of this house."**

For Ran Zhu who had spent her life straining to be her own master, yet her span is but toil and troubles, she really want to see what it looked like for someone not to live as their own master, but to live and move and have their being in Christ, and what their end would be.

Ran Zhu took a job in the product development department of a battery and energetic devices designer and manufacturer company, it is an American-owned and operated battery technology company that makes batteries by utilizing the most advanced technology and innovative processes. Ran Zhu worked product development department responsible for development work on the thermal battery technology which are primarily used in military and space applications requiring a one-time use power source. Ran Zhu worked company manufactures and develops thermal batteries are ideal suited for military application due to their maintenance-free, long shelf life and high power that can operate in extreme temperature ranges and climates, became the leading thermal battery manufacturer in a wide variety of military applications including missiles, munitions, torpedoes, ejection seats, guidance systems, sonobuoys and lunch vehicles. Because battery production could tolerate no contamination, and temperature and humidity had to remain strictly controlled, no objects other than equipment, materials, and authorized staff were permitted in the production room. Each entry was through an airlock, employees entered the first door, donned sterilized white coats like hospital doctors, pulled on baker-style caps, masks, gloves, and shoe covers, and only then opened the second door into the production room. In addition to research and development, Ran Zhu's job also required testing various batteries against their standards in various production rooms. With only thirty minutes for lunch, ten minutes were lost suiting up and removing gear, and another ten in the restroom, leaving barely enough time to eat. So she simply gave up lunch altogether. The company's employees were immigrants from different nations, locals typically worked in government or large domestic firms, seldom in foreign companies, and rarely in technical or manual jobs, if at all, usually in management. Immigrants, however, struggled to integrate into local circles, clinging instead to their own languages, cultures, and ideologies. Worse still, many from poorer, politically repressed, or culturally stunted countries harbored irrational hostility toward other immigrants. Often concealed, such hostility flared at the smallest spark. And if such a person gained power, however small, it often became a nightmare for those under them. Having been forced to bow to authority in their homelands, they craved power intensely. Once in power, they frequently abused it, naively assuming others should obey them as they once obeyed. When they met resistance, their fragile pride turned to injury and rage. By skipping lunch, Ran Zhu also skipped the key social circle of workplace bonding, the gossip, the chatter, she was already marked as different, plus Ran Zhu openly declared that she lived her live and move and have her being to please the Lord, not to please men, and Ran Zhu refused the COVID vaccine, all these became sparks for conflict. By skipping lunch, Ran Zhu also skipped the hassle of having to queue up to enter each production room after lunch, and usually Ran Zhu entered earlier than others to the production room. A colleague who had joined at the same time as Ran Zhu was promoted to team leader, on her first day in the new role, returned the production room after lunch while Ran Zhu was already inside the production room. She asked Ran Zhu what she was doing there, but as more employees entered, the temperature and humidity controls kicked in with a roar, the air-conditioning system noise drowned out her muffled voice behind the mask. Ran Zhu, listening to music through one earphone, heard nothing. The small authority of the new leader took a deep wound. She went straight to the manager to complain. The manager came, discovered Ran Zhu's earphone, and forbade listening to music at work. Ran Zhu didn't take it seriously, and this enraged the manager, who loved wielding power over trifles. With multiple offenses, earphone at work, no COVID vaccine, and insubordination, the manager reported Ran Zhu to head office, and the HR department approved, so Ran Zhu was dismissed.

羽化

Chapter 4   Emergence

"We were buried therefore with him by baptism into death, in order that, just as Christ was raised from the dead by the glory of the Father, we too might walk in newness of life"
(Romans 6:4)

Ran Jingming died on Christmas Day, the day of universal rejoicing. Death often stirs human reflection. Ran Zhu began to consider seriously: should she continue on the same path of life as before, or begin an entirely new way? The first leads only to death; the second aroused her curiosity as an observer, and she resolved to explore it. Ran Zhu began with a short-term mission trip to Ecuador. The family running the guesthouse was very warm. The hostess, a retired English teacher, managed most of the business, while her husband, who spoke only Spanish, handled room maintenance. Their son, a tour guide, often took Ran Zhu and the others sightseeing when he had free time. On the equator line, Ran Zhu managed to balance an egg upright and received an "Equator Egg Certificate." Standing with her feet straddling the equatorial marker—"0°0′0″"—she saw that on her left, in the Southern Hemisphere, the water in a basin drained clockwise; on her right, in the Northern Hemisphere, the water drained counterclockwise. Ran Zhu reflected on the human condition: whether one encounters smooth or adverse circumstances often depends on one's conduct on a single thought tipping the balance. To follow the purity, compassion, and humility within the heart is to walk the road of light, where things prosper; to rebel against the good within and act willfully is to live in darkness, bringing ruin upon oneself. At Chimborazo, the point on the earth's surface farthest from the center of the planet, Ran Zhu, for the first time, came close to her own heart. She realized she had never truly cared for her heart, never spoken with it, never considered its feelings. She had let it go hungry and cold. With gratitude, she finally began to feed it with the bread of life, so that it was instructed in the Lord's way and burned with holy fire. What she loved most about the equatorial land that were the butterflies, brightly colored, endlessly varied. They, in turn, seemed to love her, often alighting quietly on her hair, her clothes, her outstretched arms, and even upon her open Bible. There she read, "Therefore, if anyone is in Christ, he is a new creation. The old has passed away; behold, the new has come" *(2 Corinthians 5:17)*. Ran Zhu thought about life on earth: like a pupa wrapped in its cocoon. Death is like the disappearance of the husk when the butterfly breaks free. In truth, life does not vanish—it is transformed into a new and more beautiful life.

Du Zhi died during the global outbreak of the COVID-19 pandemic. Disasters often reveal the true nature of humanity. After being dismissed from her company, Ran Zhu, without a vaccination card was unable to receive any government subsidies. With expenses piling up, Ran Zhu knew she had to find a job quickly to survive, to prove her faith, and to endure so as to receive the unfading crown of glory. What she did not know was that more trials were already assembling in ranks, the battle was coming.

Because of fear of infection, many people were unwilling to go out to work, Ran Zhu discovered that many construction sites were in urgent need of laborers, and since the work was outdoors, vaccination cards were not strictly required. After sending her résumé to several construction companies, she quickly received multiple offers. Suddenly enlightened, a brand-new plan began to form in her mind. Ran Zhu reached out to several fellow new immigrants in New Zealand who, caught in the pandemic, had also been unable to find work, she asked each of them to contact others in the same situation, and very quickly Ran Zhu had gathered a team of more than twenty workers. Ran Zhu's company signed contracts with several general contractors. The construction companies paid her company NZ$32 per hour per worker, while she paid her own laborers NZ$18 per hour. As the pandemic waned and the economy began to recover, with greater mobility of people, the real estate sector was the first to sense opportunity and launch new development projects. Business for Ran Zhu's company flourished. Yet, ***"Pride goes before destruction,*** *and a haughty spirit before a fall" (Proverbs 16:18).* As her success grew, so did her boasting and arrogance. She forgot the reminder of God's Word: *"For who sees anything different in you? What do you have that you did not receive? If then you received it, why do you boast as if you did not receive it?" (1 Corinthians 4:7)*

Ran Zhu's company was a subcontractor for construction labor. Besides supplying workers and arranging assignments, she was required to attend the general contractor's daily meetings to understand the site's progress, the coordination needed among subcontractors, and most important of all was safety issues. Sometimes subcontractor heads were even required to attend mandatory safety training sessions so they could pass it on to their teams. That year the weather was strange; that day the meeting atmosphere was even stranger. The safety officer of the general contractor briefly reported that a worker had died from a fall the previous day. He gave no details about the cause, only demanded that all subcontractor leaders attend mental health first aid training that day. After the session, Ran Zhu needed fresh air. Ran Zhu stood on the 52nd floor, and for some reason suddenly recalled the lines from the film "*Manhunt*', Du Qiu, look, the sky is so blue. Walk over, and you can dissolve into the sky, just keep walking, don't look to either side, do you understand? Du Qiu, hurry up, go!"Ran Zhu laughed out loud for no apparent reason, in the empty floor, the echo of her laughter became eerie, chilling her with sweat. The wind roared louder and louder, her head buzzed, then thundered deafeningly. Ran Zhu did not remember how she walked over to dissolve into the sky, she only remembered, as her body fell, that it seemed a great force held her up; then came a dull pain sweeping through her body, and she lost consciousness.

A male and a female police officer took shifts at her bedside until she awoke. They questioned her in detail, recording everything. The male police officer told Ran Zhu that his parents had come from Shenyang, and he had seen how their generation struggled under cultural dislocation, so he knew the hardship of first-generation immigrants. Seeing Ran Zhu stirred his compassion deeply. He told Ran Zhu more than required: that as Ran Zhu fell, because the building was so high and the wind so strong, as she was thin, her fall from the fifty-second floor had been blown sideways, so that she landed upon the terrace of the forty-seventh floor. There, amidst a forest of exposed rebar, one bar was missing its protective safety cap, piercing her abdomen. Among high-rise fall cases, Ran Zhu's survival was extraordinarily rare, so the male police officer sincerely hoped that Ran Zhu spared from death, would live well. Miracles often remind humanity of its insignificance. Ran Zhu knew deeply that if it had not been the God who created heaven and earth, with His mighty arm stretched out to protect her, she would long ago have returned to dust.

When the doctor came for his rounds, he asked Ran Zhu with kindness how she felt. Ran Zhu tried to sit up to inquire about her injuries, but stabbing pain bent her double, drenching her in sweat. The doctor explained that she was indeed very fortunate, the rebar that pierced her abdomen had missed her intestines, so no surgery was needed to clean the cavity, there was slight damage to her liver, but since the liver has strong regenerative capacity, she could recover. Ran Zhu refused the painkillers the nurse offered. Bodily pain distracted her from the wounds of the heart. She knew her offense she had sinned against the God who gave her life. Without His presence, her world lay desolate. Ran Zhu's heart was empty and barren, and Ran Zhu's wealth could not save her. She knew this had come upon her because of her pride, her boasting. Even slight movement left her dizzy and gasping; blood loss was great, each day when nurses measured her blood pressure, they ordered her to lie flat, lest she faint. Her blood tests were filled with red warning marks. She lived each day in pain and sorrow, convinced she could never return to what she had been. Exhausted in body and soul, she opened the Bible she had long neglected, it happens to be1 John 2:15–17,

"Do not love the world or the things in the world. If anyone loves the world, the love of the Father is not in him. For all that is in the

world, the desires of the flesh and the desires of the eyes and the pride of life is not from the Father but is from the world. And the world is passing away along with its desires, but whoever does the will of God abides forever". Like a guilty child before a stern yet merciful Father, she prayed, *"Have mercy on me, O God, according to your steadfast love; according to your abundant mercy blot out my transgressions...Cast me not away from your presence, and take not your Holy Spirit from me... a broken and contrite heart, O God, you will not despise."* (Psalm 51:1, 11, 17b) *"Look away from me, that I may smile again, before I depart and am no more!"* (Psalm 39:13).

Ran Zhu, who had miraculously survived, had also miraculously recovered. The birds' singing, the sunlight filtering through the trees, and the plants inhaling carbon dioxide and releasing oxygen filled Ran Zhu with a sense of peace during her morning run. Ran Zhu decided to equip herself at a seminary to constantly remind herself of her Savior, Jesus Christ who though He was in the form of God, gave himself as a ransom for all, became flesh into the world in the likeness of man to save her and all people from their sins, He bled and died on the cross, cleansing all sin and making peace by the blood of His cross so that all things could be through Him to reconciled with God, According to His great mercy, He has caused those who have believed in God to be born again to a living hope through the resurrection of Jesus Christ from the dead, and be set them free in Christ Jesus from the bondage of sin. To help more people hear this precious truth and live as God originally intended revering God and shunning evil; respecting life and ceasing to harm one another, as we are all created in God's image; learning to be grateful and to share, while avoiding all resentment, hypocrisy, deceit, wickedness, greed, malice, jealousy, and strife Ran Zhu resolved to treat others with sincere compassion, kindness, humility, gentleness, and patience.

At the seminary, Ran Zhu diligently equipped herself with God's word, ready to be sent by Him at any time. Upon graduation, she began her missionary journey. Looking out the window, Ran Zhu saw herself above the clouds, mount up with wings like eagles.

Epilogue

"I have considered my ways and have turned my steps to your statutes" (Psalm 119:59)

Among the Chinese immigrant community, there is always the inward sense of being sojourners without belonging, without cultural identity ,　much like the Israelites in the Old Testament. Even though the LORD their God was giving them, a land flowing with milk and honey, as the LORD their God has promised them, still they wandered in desert wastes. Yet those who hold fast to their faith confess that they are strangers and exiles on the earth. And the holy ones of the Most High will be richly provided for you an entrance into the eternal kingdom of our Lord and Savior Jesus Christ, to be His people forever and ever.